Cupcakes and Corpses

Pupcakes and Peril

Paige Tyler

Copyright © 2025 by Paige Tyler

All rights reserved.

No part of this publication may be reproduced, distributed, or transmitted in any form or by any means, including photocopying, recording, or other electronic or mechanical methods, without the prior written permission of the publisher, except as permitted by U.S. copyright law.

The story, all names, characters, and incidents portrayed in this production are fictitious. No identification with actual persons (living or deceased), places, buildings, and products is intended or should be inferred.

Cover Image by Anastasia

Editing by Jennifer Jakes/The Killion Group

Proofreading by RVP

With special thanks to my extremely patient and understanding husband, without whose help and support I couldn't have pursued my dream job of becoming a writer. You're my sounding board, my idea man, my critique partner, and the absolute best research assistant any girl could ask for!
Thank you!

Chapter 1

Having a party outdoors in the spring in Maine was tricky. It could be cold and rainy or warm and sunny. Luckily for Tassie Drake, the weather for the baby shower she was hosting for her best friend, Lucy Shaw, was a balmy sixty degrees. Well, balmy by New England standards anyway.

Which—in her opinion—meant not having to bundle up in a winter coat and knit cap. Today, she was wearing a lightweight gray sweater dress and knee-high leather boots, so it was all good.

From where she stood on the covered deck sipping her iced tea, Tassie surveyed the dozens of pink and white balloons, pastel-colored streamers, and baby animal decorations that she and her sister, Abby, had set up around Lucy's backyard. Completely fenced in, it was the perfect size to entertain the two dozen guests, as well as their dogs, who were having as much fun as their pet parents.

And best of all, no one had tried to kill anyone.

Yet.

Not that there were a lot of murders in Bluewater Bay, of course. Unless you counted the one that had happened a few weeks ago when someone had killed the meanest get-off-my-lawn old man in their small town. Not many people had shed a tear, Tassie included. But then, to the shock of everyone, her friend had been arrested for the crime and Tassie had made it her mission to clear Sara's name. Much to the consternation of the town's handsome new detective. At least until he'd realized she was rather good at the whole sleuthing thing—something that had kind of surprised her too. Apparently, all those hours watching *Murder She Wrote* and the plethora of movies on the Hallmark Mystery Channel were time well spent.

Thankfully, along with the help of her adorable Chiweenie, Baxter, she'd discovered the real murderer and had finally been able to get back to planning Lucy's baby shower. Unfortunately, she wasn't enjoying most of it at the moment because she was too busy keeping an eye on Gwen Swanson and Irene Bartlett.

Tassie sipped her iced tea again, gaze drifting in their direction where the two women stood sizing each other up as only the two of them could seem to do.

Gwen was the owner of The Cupcakery, which was right next door to Pupcakes, the doggy bakery Tassie co-owned with Abby. Irene was the owner of Dreamy Desserts, located a few stores down and on the other side of the street. Even though Gwen's bakery specialized in cupcakes while Irene made everything from cookies to pie to the most delicious, moist, decadent chocolate cake on the planet, the two of them were always in competition. It had been like that since they were in high school.

Tassie should know because she'd been friends with both of them since then.

To make matters worse, Gwen and Irene would be going up against each other in a huge baking contest in a few days. As a result, their rivalry was more intense than ever.

From the way Gwen was glaring at Irene—and Irene at Gwen—at the moment, Tassie fully expected her friends to start throwing the cupcakes they'd brought to the party at each other before the guests even had a chance to taste them. And those cupcakes were way too delicious looking to end up being innocent victims in a food fight. Especially not with those super cute teddy bear decorations sitting on top of all that delectable frosting.

Nope.

A food fight was not happening.

Not on her watch.

Baxter regarded her from where he sat on the lawn beside her. Black with some caramel, he had a patch of white right on his chin that made it look like he was smiling whenever he looked up at you. Right now, it made Tassie suspect he might think a food fight could be fun—especially if he and his fellow doggy friends at the party got to snack on the fallout.

"Still not happening," she told him with a grin.

Resigned—and probably a little disappointed too—Baxter turned his attention back to the party, watching Bruno, Lucy's Basset Hound, sniff the ground for any crumbs of food he could find, his long ears brushing the grass as he walked.

"Ready to find out what Lucy and Andrew are going to name the baby?"

Tassie turned to see Abby standing there, an excited look on her face, her cute brown Dachshund, Finn, at her side. Older than Tassie's twenty-five by a couple years, Abby wore her hair in a braid over one shoulder along with a long colorful sweater paired with black leggings and boots.

Drats.

Tassie had almost forgotten about the cockamamie idea that Lucy and her husband, Andrew, had come up with to have the guests pick a name for the baby since they couldn't agree on any of them. She and Abby had tried to talk them out of it, saying it was fraught with all kinds of danger. Like someone picking a name Lucy and Andrew absolutely hated. Or a name that wasn't a name at all. Such as Lemonade, or something like that. But Lucy assured her it would be fine.

So, they were doing this.

"Did you take out all the weird names?" Tassie asked, pushing her long, light brown hair over her shoulder.

Was it right to remove them? Maybe not. But someone had to look out for her goddaughter otherwise the poor girl could go through life with a name that was a string of Greek letters with a hyphen somewhere in between.

Abby nodded and held out the bowl of folded index cards. "Streamer, Tangerine, and Corduroy are officially out of the running."

Someone suggested Lucy and Andrew name their little girl *Corduroy?*

Seriously?

Shaking her head, Tassie gave her sister grateful a smile as she took the bowl. "You are a lifesaver. Thank you." She glanced at Baxter. "Okay, let's go find Lucy and Andrew."

They were over by the gift table, talking to Estelle Nichols, Bluewater Bay's resident historian, and purveyor of all things gossipy.

Petite with shoulder-length dark curly hair, Lucy was the definition of glowing, while her tall, cute firefighter husband was the epitome of proud daddy-to-be.

"Tassie!" Estelle said. A little shorter than Lucy, her dark hair was touched with gray, and she wore big, round glasses. "You did a lovely job with the party! The food is delicious and the decorations are perfect!"

Tassie grinned. "Thank you. I couldn't have done it without Abby's and Lucy's help, though." She glanced down at her fur baby. "And Baxter, too."

Estelle laughed along with Lucy and Andrew, then bent to give Baxter a pet. "Of course."

Lucy eagerly eyed the bowl Tassie held. "Is that what I think it is?"

"It is," Tassie said. "Are you guys ready to pick your baby's name?"

"You know it!" Lucy said.

Beside her, Andrew didn't look nearly as enthusiastic. In fact, he seemed a little anxious.

Tassie was right there with him. Even so, she gathered all the guests around, announcing they'd be picking the baby's name. Everyone hurried over to see if theirs was the one chosen. Even Gwen and Irene stopped glowering at each other to join in.

Grinning, Tassie held the bowl out to Lucy and Andrew. "Who wants to do the honors?"

Lucy and Andrew exchanged looks. Hers was full of anticipation while his seemed more like it was leaning toward trepidation.

"You pick," Andrew said to Lucy.

She eagerly stuck her hand in the bowl, swirling it around in the sea of folded index cards.

"This is so exciting!" Estelle exclaimed.

A moment later, Lucy pulled out an index card and raised it above her head triumphantly.

Tassie held her breath, unable to help it. Beside her, even Baxter seemed a little nervous.

Taking a deep breath, Lucy unfolded the card and her face immediately lit up.

"Our little girl's name is…" Lucy gave her husband a big smile. "Flower!"

Rose Adams, the blonde woman in the bright floral print palazzo pants and white top, who was standing near Estelle, jumped up and down, clapping her hands. "Yay! That's my pick!"

Squealing, Rose ran over to hug Lucy. As Bluewater Bay's local floral genius and owner of Bloom Boutique Florist, it made sense that she'd choose Flower.

Andrew leaned over to Tassie. "I don't hate the name," he said softly from behind his hand. "Actually, I kind of like it."

She nodded, relief flooding through her. "Me too! It's pretty!"

Lucy hurried over to wrap her arms around Andrew, gushing about how much she loved the name, then hugged Tassie tightly.

"See?" Lucy said. "I told you that our friends and family would suggest beautiful names!"

Tassie laughed. "You did!"

And Lucy never needed to know that she tossed the names Streamer, Tangerine, and Corduroy. Although, she was definitely going to hold onto those names to one day in the future let her goddaughter, Flower, know what fate she'd save her from.

"I'm going to grab something to drink," Andrew said as everyone went back to what they were doing before Lucy picked their baby's name. "Do you want anything, hon? Tassie?"

"I'll take some iced ginger tea," Lucy said.

Tassie smiled. "I'm good, thanks."

"So," Lucy said slowly. "You and Jack."

As in Jack Sterling, Bluewater Bay's handsome new detective. The one who made her smile and feel warm all over every time she thought about him. They'd met at a crime scene because she and Baxter had been lucky—or unlucky, she supposed—enough to find that meanest get-off-my-lawn old man's body. Lucy had joked that nothing said romance like crime scene tape and chalk outlines. While Tassie wasn't so sure about that, there'd definitely been some sparks between her and Jack.

"What about Jack and me?" she asked coyly.

"When are the two of you going on a date?"

"Does running into each other at the dog park count?"

The look Lucy gave her said it all.

Tassie laughed. "I know. I know. I don't think it counts either. As it turns out, I might have something to report on that front in the very near future." She grinned giddily, unable to contain her excitement. "Jack asked me if I'd like to go out to dinner with him after the cupcake baking contest."

Lucy was the one who let out a squeal this time. "Yes! I want a full detailed report after your date. And you'd better not leave anything out!"

"I won't," Tassie said with another laugh. "Promise."

She would have said more, but then she caught sight of Gwen and Irene. They'd gone back to the deck and were both standing by their respective trays of cupcakes like they were guarding them. And while Tassie couldn't hear what they were saying, the expressions on their faces suggested they were going to start arguing any minute.

"I better get over there and play referee before Gwen and Irene start throwing cupcakes at each other," she said.

Lucy followed her gaze, letting out a groan. "Let me know if you need any help."

Assuring her that she would, Tassie scooped Baxter up in her arms.

"Okay, let's go do an intervention," she told her fur baby, determinedly making her way over to where the dessert table was set up on the deck.

"Clearly everyone prefers my cupcakes to yours," Gwen said proudly as she gave Irene's tray a disdainful look. Petite with blonde hair, her blue eyes shot daggers. "I told you that no one can resist chocolate and peanut butter, especially when you pair them together in a moist chocolate cupcake filled with gooey peanut butter and topped with heaps of fluffy frosting."

Irene let out a delicate snort. "Not everyone. My chocolate cupcakes with a hint of rosemary and topped with blackberry buttercream are way more popular than yours. Anyone can see that."

Tassie looked from one tray to the other, forcing herself to focus on doing some quick math instead of how perfectly yummy both varieties looked. By her count, there were exactly the same number of cupcakes on both trays. She doubted Gwen and Irene would agree even if she added the sweet treats up in front of them.

"Okay, ladies. Let's keep it friendly," Tassie said, giving each of them a smile. "This is Lucy's special day, remember? I'm sure both your cupcakes are as delicious as they look. And I for one can't wait to try them!"

Gwen and Irene both appeared contrite at that, even if they did still stare daggers at one another.

"You're right," Gwen said, smoothing her hair.

Irene nodded, her strawberry blonde ponytail bouncing. "Sorry. *Cupcake Combat* is in a few days. I guess we're both already in competition mode."

Tassie resisted the urge to roll her eyes. What else was new? Gwen and Irene were *always* in competition mode. From where he chilled in Tassie's arms, Baxter gave her a look that said he was thinking the same thing.

"Although," Irene said, gaze sliding slyly to Gwen. "You might not want to make those signature cupcakes of yours for the baking contest since Juniper is deathly allergic to peanut butter."

Juniper Larabee had a YouTube channel where she shared baking tips and recipes specifically for people who had a peanut allergy like she did. Since she was something of a celebrity in her own right in Bluewater Bay, the TV show *Cupcake Combat* asked her to be one of the judges for the contest. That meant all of the cupcakes had to be peanut-free.

"I wouldn't want you killing her," Irene added sweetly.

Tassie cringed. Another murder was all Bluewater Bay needed. Though that was kind of a low blow from Irene about the peanut butter.

It was at that moment that Tassie decided that she had a new mission in life. As soon as the *Cupcake Combat* show was over and done with, she was going to get Gwen and Irene in a room together and she wasn't going to let them out until they remembered that they used to be best friends. This cupcake-fueled animosity was stupid and needed to end!

Chapter 2

Tassie had never been to the taping of a TV show before. She'd be lying if she said she wasn't excited about being part of the audience. Especially since *Cupcake Combat* was one of her favorite shows. It was true. If she wasn't solving mysteries on the Hallmark Channel, she was vicariously baking with the pastry chefs on the Dessert Network.

The people from the show had transformed the town's seaside park into a festive area with colorful tents, tables filled with dry baking ingredients and stand mixers, fridges, stovetops, and even portable ovens. Along with the three mini-kitchens, they'd also set up a table for the judges as well as loads of seating for the audience. Not surprisingly, there was a large crowd, along with Tassie and Baxter also eagerly waiting to watch the competition as well as taste the contestants' cupcakes. Not to mention, see the famous star judges in action, including Bluewater Bay's attention-seeking

CUPCAKES AND CORPSES 13

mayor, who was gripping and grinning and puffing out his chest like no one's business.

It was fascinating to see how many people diligently worked behind the scenes to make a baking show like this happen. In addition to the crew responsible for the sound and lighting equipment, there seemed to be an army of people making sure that all the ingredients were ready and waiting for the bakers competing in the contest. Tassie was exhausted just watching them.

Sitting on her lap, Baxter was just as captivated by the whole production as she was.

"I didn't miss anything, did I?"

Tassie turned her head to see Jack slipping into the seat she'd been saving for him, two cardboard to-go cups from Hug in a Mug, Bluewater Bay's coffee shop, in his hands. Tall with dark hair, dreamy brown eyes, a square jaw with that perfect amount of stubble, and broad shoulders, he looked like he should be in front of the camera instead of sitting in the audience. Well, maybe not on a baking show. No, she pictured him playing the lead in some kind of action movie. Or maybe a police detective in one of the mysteries she liked watching on Hallmark.

Oh, yes! Definitely that!

She smiled at him as he reached out to pet Baxter, who greeted him with a wagging tail. "Nope. They're still doing all the pre-show stuff."

"Good. I had some paperwork to finish up and was afraid I'd be late." Grinning, he held out one of the cups.

"Cinnamon chai tea, two packs of sweetener. That's your drink, right?"

Handsome *and* thoughtful. "It is. Thank you." She took a sip, savoring the sweet, spicy tea. "How'd you know I like cinnamon chai?"

Jack's mouth twitched. "A detective never reveals his sources."

"I'm pretty sure that's a reporter," she said with a laugh.

That earned her a deep chuckle. "Aria told me. I explained that I was meeting up with you and wanted to pick up something for you since I was grabbing coffee for myself."

Aria Millikan was the owner of Hug in a Mug and knew everyone's coffee, tea, or cocoa order in town by heart.

"Ah." She smiled. "I appreciate the thought."

He sipped his coffee. "Are we still on for dinner?"

Tassie nodded, giddy at the idea. "Definitely! I'm looking forward to it."

"So am I." He reached out to pet Baxter again, who was keenly listening to their conversation. "I was thinking I could pick up Gus and we could all go to The General Store."

Gus was Jack's adorable black Lab mix and Baxter's newest bestie. Owned by a sweet older couple, The General Store was part restaurant, part grocery, part gift shop, and served the most delicious food around. Best of all, it was dog friendly.

"That's perfect," she said.

Jack held her gaze for a long minute before glancing around, taking in the pop-up kitchens and all the people moving around. "So, fill me in on the players here. I don't know anything about *Cupcake Combat*."

Tassie grinned. "Lucky for you, I do. Baxter and I watch it all the time."

"In between *Murder She Wrote* and those Hallmark Mysteries of course," he teased.

"Of course," she agreed with a laugh, then pointed to a gray-haired man standing by the main table looking at his cell phone. "That's Pierre Bardot. He's *Cupcake Combat's* resident judge and renowned French pastry chef. He's not a fan of red velvet cupcakes, but every other show one of the bakers makes them anyway. I don't know why." She pointed again, this time at a woman with dark blonde, shoulder-length hair. "And that's Mia Jones, the show's other resident judge. She's the owner of the famous bakery *I Love Cake* in New York City. She doesn't like a lot of frosting on cupcakes, though, which I don't get. The frosting is the best part."

Jack snorted. "I can't argue with you there."

"I know, right? I think I'd eat a dog biscuit if you put frosting on it." When Baxter gave her a look, she kissed him on the top of the head. "You know it's true," she told him before giving Jack a shrug. "Other than that, they're both easygoing and complimentary and never embarrass the bakers or anything like that."

It was one of the reasons Tassie loved the show. She didn't like watching the cooking shows—or any competition show honestly—where the judges constantly yelled or belittled the people, whether it was drama manufactured solely for the show or not.

"What's really fun about *Cupcake Combat* is that the show films all over the U.S. and Canada," she continued excitedly. "So, they always choose someone from the town or city they're in who's in the culinary world to be the third judge, like someone who owns a bakery—or is an internet influencer. The red-haired woman in the black sequin top standing over there taking a video of herself on her bedazzled phone is Juniper Larabee, Bluewater Bay's famous YouTube baker and local celebrity judge for the show. She has like a million followers. She also had a severe peanut allergy, so all the cupcakes need to be peanut-free, which is a first in the history of *Cupcake Combat*."

Beside Tassie, Jack regarded her in amazement and maybe a little awe. "Wow. You really do know a lot about this show."

"I know a lot about a lot of stuff," she teased.

He chuckled. "I'm starting to learn that about you." He gestured to the kitchen area of the set with his coffee cup. "What do you know about the bakers who are competing?"

"Well," she began. "Hazel Dutton, the gray-haired woman at the center kitchen, is a home baker who's won almost every baking contest at the town's summer and winter festivals since before I was born."

"So, she's the favorite then?"

Tassie considered that. "Not necessarily. Gwen and Irene both own bakeries, so I think they'll give Hazel a run for her money. If they don't kill each other first."

She glanced over at Graham Bartlett where he sat across the aisle from them. Irene's older brother, he had a slim build and curly red hair. Oh, and he also had the biggest crush on Gwen. She felt the same about him, Tassie was sure of it, but because he didn't want to hurt his sister, he refused to act on that attraction and ask Gwen out.

"Oh, that's right," Jack said, his gaze going to where Gwen and Irene stood with Hazel in the kitchen getting last-minute instructions. "The two bakers who used to be friends but are now arch enemies. They didn't turn the baby shower into a food fight, did they?"

"Not quite." She made a face. "But they did spend most of it glaring at each other and debating which of their cupcakes was better. If either one of them wins *Cupcake Combat*, they'll never let the other hear the end of it."

"So you're hoping Hazel wins."

She cringed. "Is it bad if I say yes?"

"I think it's smart if you say yes. Especially if you always get in the middle of their fights," he told her. "That said, who do you think *will* win?"

She blew out a breath, making her bang flutter. "Oh, that's a tough one. Gwen's specialty is cupcakes and they're always a hit. But Irene's creativity and determination to outdo Gwen might give her an edge. And when it comes to Hazel, you can never count out the experience she has not only when it comes to baking but competing too."

"Maybe they should have picked you to be the local celebrity judge."

She laughed. "I'll stick to doggy treats, thank you very much."

Baxter booped her nose in agreement.

"I guess Baxter thinks so too," Jack said with a chuckle.

Tassie opened her mouth to answer, but the audience coordinator, a young guy with glasses and curly dark hair announced that the show was starting. Promising herself she'd fill Jack in on the baby shower later, she cuddled Baxter and kissed the top of his head even as he sniffed around, excited by all the new scents.

"Are you excited to watch one of our favorite shows in person, baby?" she whispered.

In answer, he half turned and gave her nose a sideways boop with his, then turned his attention to the action happening in front of them, watching raptly as the smiling host of the show, Michael Brisco, greeted the camera.

"Today, we're in the beautiful seaside town of Bluewater Bay, Maine, where three exceptional bakers will face off to win ten thousand dollars and ultimate bragging rights of *Cupcake Combat* Champion!"

Tassie clapped and cheered along with the rest of the people in the audience, listening raptly as Michael introduced the show's judges and each of the competitors, telling everyone a little about them.

CUPCAKES AND CORPSES   19

Watching the show in person was even more fun than on TV. Okay, some of that probably had to do with the fact that she personally knew the bakers competing. Watching them make cupcakes in the allotted time was surprisingly nerve-wracking. But Gwen, Irene, and Hazel kept their wits about them as they mixed batter and made frosting even as each of their respective assistants created decorations to really make their cupcakes stand out. And all that while Pierre, Mia, and Juniper discussed and critiqued what they were doing.

By the time Michael announced that time was up and the show took its first "commercial" break, Tassie was on the edge of her seat.

As Pierre and Mia answered audience questions during the break, Tassie leaned over to Jack. "Having fun?"

Jack grinned. "I am. Though I have to admit, I'm more interested in the company than the cupcakes."

Tassie blushed and laughed. She couldn't agree more. The company was pretty great from her point of view too.

"One minute, everyone!" the production assistant announced.

As everyone scrambled back to their places, the make-up artists did some quick touch-ups on Pierre, Mia, and Michael as well as the competitors. Juniper insisted on doing her own makeup, meticulously applying a fresh coat of shiny lip gloss as her assistant, Victoria Farris, held up a mirror for her. Apparently, being a famous YouTuber had turned her into quite the diva.

"Welcome back to *Cupcake Combat*," Michael announced with a smile the moment the cameras were rolling again. "It's time for the bakers to present their first-round cupcakes. Hazel, if you'll please describe what you've made for the judges."

From where she stood in front of their table, Hazel gave Pierre, Mia, and Juniper what could only be called a confident smile. "I've prepared coconut macaroon cupcakes inspired by the classic macaroon. It's a moist coconut cupcake, topped with a delicate coconut meringue frosting, and covered with toasted coconut. I hope you enjoy them as much as my family does."

They sounded absolutely yummy to Tassie—and looked it. She couldn't wait until the audience got to try the cupcakes after the show finished taping. She was definitely snagging one of those coconut babies.

At the judges' table, Pierre, Mia, and Juniper inspected the cupcake, studying it from all angles before remarking on how beautiful it looked. Picking up their forks, they each slowly cut into their cupcakes. That was one thing about the show that drove Tassie crazy. Maybe it was the little kid in her, but eating a cupcake with your hands was half the fun. Although, if they were anything like her, they'd end up getting frosting on their face, and that probably wouldn't be very good for the camera.

From Juniper's expression after tasting the macaroon cupcake, she must have thought it was delicious. "Hazel, these cupcakes are..."

At first, Tassie thought Juniper hesitated because she was searching for the right word, but then the woman's hand flew to her throat as she struggled to breathe. She pushed back the chair, trying to stand, only to wobble and fall to the dais while Pierre, Mia, and Michael stared in disbelief.

"She's going into anaphylactic shock!"

Victoria's panicked words rang out in the park as she ran up to the dais, Juniper's purse in hand.

Beside Tassie, Jack was already on his feet and headed in that direction, cell phone to his ear as he called for an ambulance. Tassie hurried after him, Baxter in her arms. By the time they got to the dais, Victoria had dug Juniper's epinephrine auto-injector out of her purse and was administering the drug.

"It's not working!" Victoria cried.

Jack dropped to a knee beside Victoria. Tassie noted how amazingly calm he was despite the chaos going on all around him. "Does Juniper carry a second auto-injector?"

"I..." Victoria stared at him in confusion, then something dawned on her face. "Yes!"

Scrambling for Juniper's purse, she dumped it out until she found the second auto-injector. Grabbing it, she shoved it against Juniper's skin. "It still isn't working!"

Jack felt for a pulse at Juniper's neck, then immediately performed CPR while Tassie held her breath. He continued with the chest compressions until the paramedics showed up to take over. After what seemed like an eternity, the man also felt for a pulse then sat back on his heels and looked up at Tassie and Jack and the rest of the people who had gathered around.

"Juniper's dead."

Chapter 3

Tassie's head spun. Behind her, a collective gasp echoed through the crowd of people in the park before everyone started talking among themselves all at once. Pierre, Mia, Michael, and the rest of the crew from *Cupcake Combat* appeared equally stunned.

How could Juniper be dead?

The woman was just touching up her makeup and primping for the camera not five minutes ago. If she'd gone into anaphylactic shock that meant she had an allergic reaction to eating something made with peanuts. But all she'd eaten was...

Hazel's cupcake.

Tassie looked over at the older woman standing a few feet away with her baking assistant, studying them thoughtfully. When they'd been making the cupcakes, the show's host had mentioned that the woman was Hazel's sister, Charlotte. Not that Tassie needed anyone to tell her that they were sisters. With chestnut hair graying in places and dark eyes, they looked like they could have been twins. Both of them looked beside themselves right now.

Who could blame them? Juniper had died after eating the cupcakes they'd made.

Had Hazel deliberately put peanuts in the cupcakes knowing it would kill Juniper? That seemed too horrible to even contemplate. But murder had happened in Bluewater Bay before.

Quite recently, too.

Not that Tassie was saying what happened to Juniper was murder, of course.

It could simply have been a terrible mistake.

But if it *was* murder, what better way to kill Juniper than to make it look like an accident?

But why would Hazel want Juniper dead?

Tassie wandered over to Hazel and her sister, Baxter in her arms. Hazel stood wringing her hands, her gaze locked on the barely touched cupcake on Juniper's plate.

"Hazel, this wasn't your fault," Tassie said gently.

Unless it was?

Hazel didn't even look her way, her eyes still locked on the plate. "But it was my cupcake that…"

Charlotte wrapped a comforting arm around her sister's shoulders.

"You didn't use peanuts in the cupcakes though," Tassie said. "Did you?"

Hazel looked at her then. "Of course not! Even if *Cupcake Combat* hadn't supplied all the peanut-free ingredients and baking equipment, we all knew that Juniper was allergic and would have done the same. But she went into anaphylactic shock, so how did peanuts get in there?"

How indeed?

"Come on, Hazel," Charlotte said. "Let's sit down."

Giving Tassie a small smile, Charlotte guided her sister to the closest chair, taking the one beside her, repeating what Tassie had said a few moments ago. That it wasn't Hazel's fault.

Tassie turned back to the dais, eager to get Jack's take on what might have happened, but Bluewater Bay's one and only coroner, Dr. Emmit Anthony, and his dour-faced assistant, Jameson Hall, had arrived, along with two uniformed police officers, Emily Miller and Henry Thompson.

Jack quickly instructed Emily and Henry to keep the crowd of people who had gathered around away from the dais, then focused his attention on Emmit. Trim with brown hair graying at the temples and wire-rimmed glasses, he was all kinds of socially awkward. Which probably explained why he worked with dead bodies.

Since Tassie didn't think Jack considered her and Baxter part of the crowd he wanted steering clear of the dais, she casually moved a little closer so they could listen in on his conversation with Emmit as he took the coroner through what had happened, starting with Juniper tasting the cupcake to Jack and the paramedic performing CPR. Her fur baby was just as intrigued as she was.

"I want everything tested for peanuts," Jack added.

Emmit lifted a brow. "By *everything*, you mean...?"

Jack looked around, sweeping the park with an outstretched arm. "All the stuff in Hazel's kitchen, the cupcake Juniper was eating, the glass of water she drank from, the auto-injector pens, and whatever else is in her purse. I want to know how the peanuts got into her system and why the epinephrine in those pens didn't work."

Emmit frowned. "Do you suspect foul play?"

"Just covering all the bases," Jack said noncommittally.

The coroner seemed to consider that for a moment, then nodded. "I'll have my report to you as soon as I can."

As Emmit and Jameson went about doing their jobs, Jack stepped down from the dais and walked over to where Tassie stood holding Baxter.

"I'm going to need a rain check for dinner tonight," he said, giving her an apologetic look.

She nodded. "Oh, yeah, of course."

While she understood he had to run the investigation, she was also disappointed. She'd really looked forward to their first official date. If the dejected expression on Baxter's face was any indication, he was pretty bummed, too.

"I overheard you talking to the coroner," she said. "Do you think Juniper was murdered?"

He blew out a breath. "I don't know. My gut is telling me that something is going on here, but I'm not ready to say it's murder yet. The auto-injector pens could simply be faulty."

CUPCAKES AND CORPSES

Baxter exchanged looks with Tassie. Yeah, she wasn't buying that either.

"Both of them?" she asked Jack dubiously.

"I know it's a stretch," he agreed.

"That doesn't explain how peanuts got in the cupcake," she pointed out. "Hazel said she didn't bake with anything that had peanuts in it and that the network supplied all new peanut-free baking equipment."

He regarded her thoughtfully. "Already in amateur detective mode, I see."

Tassie shrugged, giving him a little smile. "I guess my gut is telling me the same thing yours is. And you can't deny that we do make a pretty good team."

Mouth quirking, Jack reached out to pet Baxter on the head. "I wouldn't dream of it."

"Although," she added slowly. "I didn't anticipate needing to solve another murder so soon."

"We aren't sure it's murder yet," he reminded her.

She opened her mouth to concede the point, but a sharp voice cut her off.

"Detective Sterling!"

Tassie peeked around Jack to see Mayor Fillmore striding toward them with a look of consternation on his bearded face. The man walked around town like he was a feudal lord and Bluewater Bay was his fiefdom.

Jack's mouth tightened. "I'd better see what he wants. I'll text you later."

Visibly steeling himself, he turned to meet the portly man halfway.

"Mayor Fillmore," he said. "What can I help you with?"

"I want to know when *Cupcake Combat* can resume filming," Fillmore said.

Tassie cringed. Talk about too soon. The coroner and his assistant hadn't even finished moving Juniper's body yet.

"Someone really needs to read the room, don't you think, Baxter?" she muttered under her breath.

In answer, her pup turned his head and booped her nose with his.

"Come on, baby," she said. "Let's go. We have a murder to solve."

Chapter 4

Hug in a Mug, Bluewater Bay's super popular coffee shop directly across from Pupcakes lived up to its name in every sense of the word. The interior was all warm wood tones and cozy seating areas, and the whole shop was filled with the delicious scent of coffee. Even though Tassie would pick a cup of hot tea over coffee any day, she loved the aroma of the latter. Luckily, Hug in a Mug sold both.

"My usual cinnamon chai tea, a ginger tea, and a cup of whatever Detective Sterling's coffee of choice is," Tassie said when she and Baxter got to the counter.

On the other side of the polished wooden divider, Aria Millikan, the dark-haired vivacious owner of Hug in a Mug lifted a brow as she grabbed the cups and started the drinks.

"You and the good-looking detective, huh?" she said, then, when Tassie gave her a stunned look, added, "What? Yesterday, he said he was meeting up with you and wanted to buy you a drink, so he asked what your usual was. I don't have to be a detective to figure out there's something between you guys."

Tassie laughed. "Well, your method of deduction is correct. Even if I don't know how he takes his coffee yet."

"Don't worry, girl." Aria grinned. "I got you." She glanced over her shoulder as she poured the coffee. "You and Detective Sterling were at the taping of *Cupcake Combat*, right? That was awful what happened to Juniper."

"Yes," Tassie agreed. "It was quite shocking."

Aria added cream and sweetener to the coffee, then popped on a lid. "Victoria put up a tribute video to Juniper on YouTube last night. It was very moving. Fans had it trending and everything."

That was a nice thing to do, Tassie thought.

"Victoria mentioned on the video that she intends to continue the channel in Juniper's honor," Aria added as she carefully placed the cups in a sturdy cardboard drink tray. "I'm not sure if it'll work though. Juniper *was* the face of the YouTube empire."

And now Victoria was trying to step into that role. *Had she killed Juniper so she could take over and become famous?*

"I did think it was kind of weird that Victoria shot the video in Juniper's guest house where Juniper always filmed her videos," Aria said.

Maybe Victoria felt doing the video where Juniper usually filmed would make the tribute more meaningful. That said, it *was* kind of eerie in a way. Maybe also in poor taste? Tassie would have to remember to check it out to see if the woman let anything incriminating slip.

"There you go," Aria said. "One coffee, one cinnamon chai, one ginger tea, and one pup cup of freshly made whipped cream with no sugar added for your cute little baby."

Instead of putting the tiny cup in the tray, she handed it to Tassie, then leaned over the counter to give Baxter a grin. Beside Tassie, her fur baby smiled up at them, excitedly wagging his tail as he lapped up the treat.

"Baxter says thank you," Tassie told Aria with a laugh when he was finished.

"Anytime, cutie."

Tassie smiled her. "Thanks, Aria."

Picking up the tray, Tassie headed for the door, Baxter's leash in her other hand.

The lovely spring weather continued into today and a pleasant breeze coming off the water enveloped them the moment they stepped outside and started down the sidewalk, Baxter prancing along happily beside her.

Built on the coast in the late 1700s, Bluewater Bay had oodles of charm, from the historic architecture to the hand-carved wood signs. Besides Pupcakes and Hug in a Mug, there was an art gallery, ice cream parlor, and bookstore, as well as gift shops and restaurants, just to name a few of the offerings. She waved to the other shop owners as they walked, stopping to chat with some of them, much to Baxter's delight. He loved people as much as he loved his fellow dogs, so that was always a treat for him.

The police station was only a few doors down from Pupcakes so it didn't take long to get there. Emily, the uniformed officer at the counter, was on the phone when they walked in. The dark-haired woman smiled at Tassie as she and Baxter swung open the half door that divided the lobby from the main part of the station. Since Tassie stopped by to see Lucy regularly, all the cops knew her, so she pretty much had access to the bullpen area whenever her friend was working.

Lucy was at her desk, headset on, fingers tapping away at her keyboard. When she spotted Tassie and Baxter, she held up a finger, said something into her mic to the patrol officer she was talking to, then smiled and waved them over.

"Ginger tea," Tassie said, placing the cup on Lucy's desk with a smile.

"I've been craving one of these! Thank you!" Lucy picked it up and took a sip, then let out a grateful sigh. "Jack's in his office, by the way."

"What makes you think I'm here to see Jack?" Tassie asked.

Lucy looked pointedly at the tray in her hand. "Because one of those cups has coffee in it—I know because I can smell it—so unless Baxter has a caffeine addiction I don't know about, I'm thinking it must be for Jack."

Ugh. Everyone was a detective these days.

"Okay, you win," Tassie muttered. "I *am* here to see Jack."

Lucy gave her a knowing grin.

Rolling her eyes, Tassie playfully stuck out her tongue at her friend, then led Baxter over to Jack's office.

Jack was sitting at his desk—which was amazingly tidy and situated in front of the window facing the door—focused on something on his computer. Framed awards and commendations decorated the wall near the filing cabinet. Along with the letters of commendation—there were quite a few—there was also a Prestigious Service Medal, a Mayor's Achievement Medal, and a Medal for Bravery from back in Albany. She still hadn't asked him how he'd earned them, but she would.

He looked up from his computer, a grin spreading across his handsome face at the sight of her and Baxter as he got to his feet.

"Hey," he said, pushing back his chair and walking around the desk, bending to give Baxter a pet.

Tassie returned his smile. It was amazing how the guy seemingly had the unique ability to make her pulse quicken. "Since you brought me tea yesterday, I thought I'd return the favor and bring you coffee."

He took the cup she held out, grin broadening. "That was nice. Thank you."

"You're very welcome." She sipped her tea. "While I was there, Aria mentioned something interesting."

"What's that?"

"Juniper's assistant, Victoria, made a tribute video to her and had it up on YouTube a few hours after she was murdered."

"We don't know if Juniper was murdered yet," he pointed out.

She nodded. "I know. But if Juniper *was* murdered, doesn't it strike you as a little strange that her assistant put out a video that fast? It's almost like she already had it made."

Jack opened his mouth to reply but was interrupted by Emmit Anthony rushing into his office. The coroner's graying hair was sticking up like he'd just rolled out of bed, and his shirt and pants were more wrinkled than usual. Granted, she'd only seen him twice, of course, but still, this was the most unkempt she'd seen the man.

"You were right, Detective!" he said, completely ignoring Tassie and Baxter like they weren't even there as he held out a folder to Jack. "Juniper Larabee was definitely murdered and the cause of death was anaphylaxis."

Tassie knew it!

"I tested the cupcake and the wrapper first since they were the most obvious culprit and when there were no traces of peanuts, I moved on to the glass of water, plate, and fork," Emmit explained excitedly. "But it wasn't on any of those either. So next, I checked everything in her purse, starting with her makeup and I found cold-pressed peanut oil in her lip gloss. We're not talking a trace amount, either. Someone filled nearly the entire tube."

"Which meant whoever it was had access to her purse," Jack said, echoing what Tassie was already thinking. "Did you figure out why the auto-injector pens didn't work?"

Emmit nodded enthusiastically. "I did. Turns out, the killer tampered with the pens, snipping off the syringes."

Tassie exchanged looks with Baxter, who was listening to Emmit as intently as she was. That was both calculated and cold-blooded. Whoever killed Juniper wanted to make sure they got the job done.

"Any fingerprints on the lip gloss or auto-injectors?" Jack asked.

"Juniper's, of course," Emmit said. "And someone else, but I'm assuming those belong to the woman who injected her with the pens."

Jack flipped through the folder Emmit had given him, skimming the report the coroner had written. Tassie couldn't see much from where she was standing, but she caught a glimpse of a sheet of paper with an outline of a human body followed by what looked like pages upon pages of printed notes.

After a few moments, Jack gave the coroner an appraising look. "I'm impressed you were able to do all this so quickly."

Emmit positively beamed at the praise. Who knew he could be so animated?

"I've never had a chance to work on a murder investigation before. Well, other than Conrad Meyers, but that was fairly easy on my end since cause of death was so straightforward," he explained. "I stayed up all night working on Juniper Larabee's case. This is all very exciting!"

Juniper probably wouldn't agree with that, Tassie thought.

"I'd better be getting back to the morgue," Emmit said. "If you need anything else, Detective, you know where to find me!"

Giving Jack a nod, Emmit turned and left, not glancing at her and Baxter even once.

Jack dropped the file on his desk and looked at her. "Well, it looks like Hazel was telling the truth about her cupcakes being peanut-free."

Tassie thoughtfully sipped her tea. "That doesn't mean she didn't kill Juniper though."

"Agreed."

"I remember seeing Juniper applying her lip gloss during the commercial break right before the tasting," Tassie said. "She was emphatic about using her own stuff instead of letting the make-up people do it."

Jack considered that. "Question is, did whoever murdered her know she'd insist on doing her own makeup so she'd go into anaphylactic shock during the taping of the show or not? Either way, we need to narrow down who had access to her belongings, specifically her lip gloss. Did you notice anyone acting suspiciously?"

Tassie thought about that, replaying the events at the park though her head. "There was a lot going on. Gwen, Hazel, and Irene were all focused on baking, and…"

She stopped, her mind racing with possibilities.

"And what?" Jack prompted.

"I keep coming back to Juniper's assistant," she said with a sigh. "Victoria was holding Juniper's purse while the cameras were rolling. It would have been easy to slip the peanut-oil laced lip gloss into her bag. She was also the first one who raced onto the dais and made sure to use the tampered auto-injector pens from Juniper's purse."

"Then that's where we start."

"We?" she echoed.

"Yeah." His mouth curved. "You did say that we make a good team."

Yes, she did.

Chapter 5

While Jack found Victoria's address, Tassie and Baxter ran to her SUV to pick up the carrier she always used to keep her pup safe in the back seat so she could transfer it to Jack's vehicle. As often as they'd driven with Jack lately, she should seriously think about getting a second carrier and keeping it in his SUV.

A few minutes later, they were headed to Victoria's apartment. As they drove, Tassie pulled up Juniper's YouTube channel on her phone to play the tribute video Victoria had made when she realized the woman was doing a live video right then.

"Victoria is at Juniper's house, not her place," Tassie said.

Jack glanced at her. "How do you know that?"

"Because she's doing a live video and from the looks of the home, I'm pretty sure it's Juniper's guest house," she said. "At least, it appears to be the same kitchen that's in all the other videos."

Jack took out his phone and called the station to get the address. When he was finished, Tassie played the tribute video so she could watch, and he could listen while they drove. Victoria started by tearfully explaining what happened to Juniper, then saying she wanted to honor her memory by continuing Juniper's mission to bring peanut-free recipes and tips to people with allergies.

"Well, there didn't seem to be anything that points to her murdering her employer," Tassie said.

"I agree. But she seems eager to take over Juniper's business, so that's still motive."

And the fact that Victoria had access to Juniper's purse gave her ample opportunity to commit the murder. On the other hand, maybe Victoria hadn't killed Juniper at all and was simply taking advantage of the chance to be in the spotlight.

It was opportunistic and cold maybe, but certainly not criminal.

Juniper's home was a beautiful Victorian up on the cliffs overlooking the bay. With its decorative woodwork, gabled roof, and colorful stained-glass windows, it was like something out of a fairy tale.

"Wow. I could get used to this view," Jack remarked as they walked toward the smaller guest house located off to the side.

Tassie stood there for a moment, taking it all in. From here, you could see most of the town as well as the sparkling blue waters of the bay below. Charter fishing boats mingled with sailboats, kayaks, and jet skis, as well as the occasional yacht. She could even see a cruise ship in the distance. The whole scene was picture perfect.

"You and me both," Tassie said. She looked at Baxter where he was relaxing comfortably in her arms. "What about you, baby? Do you like the view?"

He booped her nose with his, making her laugh.

Leash in one hand, she set him on the paved driveway, then turned to see Jack grinning at her.

"What?" she asked.

"Nothing," he said, still smiling. "I just love watching you and Baxter interact. It's cute."

Tassie laughed. And maybe blushed a little too.

Baxter preened as he pranced along beside her.

Chuckling, Jack knocked on the door of the guest house. Since Victoria had finished her live video as they were pulling into the driveway, it was the perfect time to talk to her.

Victoria opened the door a moment later, her eyes going wide in surprise. "Detective!"

Blonde and curvy, Victoria had brown eyes and wavy auburn hair. She still had on the cute flower-print apron she'd worn in the live video Tassie had watched on the way over and she smoothed her hands over it as she looked from Jack to Tassie and back again.

"May we come in?" Jack asked.

She stepped back, opening the door wider. "Of course."

While the guest house might not be as grand as Juniper's main home, it was beautiful inside. A cozy living room greeted them as soon as they stepped inside, but the real showstopper was the big gourmet kitchen with its quartz countertops and fancy baking equipment. And the lighting and video cameras surrounding it made it feel like they were on the set of a show on the Dessert Channel.

Well, that and the delightful aroma coming from the freshly made chocolate chip muffins cooling on the counter. *Was it bad form to hope a murder suspect would offer some to her and Jack?*

"Sit," Victoria said, gesturing to the fuchsia-colored velvet sofas in the living room. "Can I get you anything to drink?"

"I'm good, thanks," Jack said, waiting until Tassie was seated on one of the couches with Baxter on her lap before sitting beside her.

Tassie smiled at Victoria. "I'm fine, thanks."

Jack looked around. "So, this is where Juniper filmed her videos."

Victoria nodded as she took a seat on the other sofa across from them, a small, sad smile curving her lips. "Yes. When she started her YouTube channel, she filmed everything in her home, but after she started making money from it, she renovated the guest house and filmed exclusively here unless she was doing a video on location or something like that."

Juniper's business had obviously been very profitable if she'd been able to do that. Well, the host of the *Cupcake Combat* show *had* introduced her as a YouTube sensation.

"How did you start working for Juniper?" Tassie asked.

"Her friend, Ada, introduced us," Victoria said. "I took all of Ada's culinary classes in high school and we kept in touch after I graduated. She knew that Juniper was looking for an assistant who knew how to cook and bake as well as had a background in social media, so Ada suggested me."

Tassie grinned, caressing Baxter's fur. "Oh, I know Ada! I took her class as an elective senior year."

Victoria's face lit up. "Ada's wonderful, isn't she?"

"She is," Tassie agreed.

It was true. Ada Cobb's class had always been a blast. Not only had she taught them how to make some seriously delicious food, she'd sprinkled in funny stories here and there that quickly made her one of Tassie's favorite teachers.

"Ada was thinking about starting a peanut-free bakery in town with Juniper," Victoria said, her gaze distant. "Now, that's never going to happen, I guess. Although, I suppose Ada might always want to open it in her memory."

"Speaking of which, we watched your tribute video to Juniper," Tassie said. "It was very moving."

Victoria nodded, taking a deep breath and letting it out slowly. "Thank you. I wanted to do what I could for her fans. Everyone loved Juniper."

Jack exchanged looks with Tassie. So did Baxter.

"Actually," he said. "Perhaps she wasn't as beloved as you thought."

Victoria frowned. "What do you mean?"

"Juniper was murdered," he said.

"What?!" Victoria's hands flew to her mouth, shock on her face. "But...how? The cupcake Hazel made?"

"It wasn't the cupcake," Tassie said.

"Someone put cold-pressed peanut oil in Juniper's lip gloss," Jack supplied.

"Cold-pressed peanut oil?" Victoria stared like she couldn't believe what she'd heard. Or was she simply stunned that they'd figured out how she killed her employer? "Juniper just did a video on that kind of oil. She talked about how dangerous it can be to people who are allergic because it has peanut protein in it, unlike refined oil. As highly allergic as she was, that kind of oil would be deadly."

Huh. It could simply be a coincidence, of course, but killing Juniper with a specific type of oil she'd recently made a video about seemed like a deliberate choice.

"But why didn't the auto-injector pens work?" Victoria asked, looking back and forth between her and Jack in what seemed like genuine confusion.

Then again, she could simply be a good actress.

"The killer snipped the syringes off," Tassie said.

If Victoria looked stunned before, she was even more astounded now. "Oh, my goodness! Who would do something like that?"

Jack exchanged another look with Tassie. As did Baxter.

"We were hoping you might be able to help us with that," he said, turning back to Victoria.

"I'm not sure how I can help, but I'll do anything I can to help you find who did this to Juniper."

Jack took a small notebook and pen out of his pocket, flipping it open to a fresh page. "Did you have Juniper's purse with you the entire time you were both in the park?"

Victoria hesitated like she was thinking back to yesterday. "She had it with her until the show started taping, then I kept it with me after that. She never liked letting her purse out of her sight since her auto-injectors were in there, but the producer didn't want anything on the dais."

Jack scribbled something in his notebook before focusing on Victoria again. "And her purse was in your possession the whole time until Juniper went into anaphylactic shock?"

Victoria fidgeted on the sofa, appearing nervous for the first time since they'd walked in. "Well, not the whole time exactly. Juniper called me over to the dais to talk to me about something and I left both our purses on my chair."

"Was that before or after she touched up her lip gloss during the commercial break?" Tassie asked.

"Before."

"Did you see anyone near her purse?" Tassie asked.

Victoria didn't say anything.

"Did you see someone, Victoria?" Jack prompted.

She still hesitated, clearly going back and forth in her mind about something. "No. But Ada was sitting next to me the whole time so maybe she saw someone."

Tassie glanced at Jack to see that he was thinking the same thing she was. Ada had access to Juniper's purse, which meant she could easily have slipped the tainted lip gloss and tampered auto-injectors into it. Tassie hated to think her former teacher was a murderer but everyone close to Juniper needed to be a suspect.

"So, the only people who had access to Juniper's purse at the taping were Ada and you then," Tassie said.

She hadn't meant the words to sound accusatory, but Victoria must have thought so because she frowned.

"Are you suggesting that I murdered Juniper?"

"Did you?" Jack asked.

Tassie held her breath, her gaze going to Baxter as she waited for Victoria's answer. He seemed to have a knack for knowing when people were lying. If they did, he'd give Tassie the side eye to let her know about it.

"There were a lot of people in the park yesterday," Victoria protested. "Any one of them could have taken her lip gloss and auto-injectors out of her bag and slipped in the tampered ones."

Well, drats. Victoria didn't deny killing Juniper so there was no way to tell if she was lying.

But as much as Tassie hated to admit it, Victoria had made some good points. Anyone could have messed with Juniper's bag.

Including Ada.

Victoria sat up straighter. "If you don't have any more questions for me, Detective, I'd like to record a video letting Juniper's fans know that she was murdered. If that's okay, I mean."

It was Jack's turn to hesitate, but after a moment, he nodded. It's not like they could keep the fact that Juniper was murdered a secret. Not when they'd be questioning potential suspects.

"As long as you don't discuss anything specific we talked about, that's fine," he said. "Thanks for your time."

Jack got to his feet. Tassie stood as well, setting Baxter on the floor.

"Do you happen to know if Juniper's husband is home?" Jack asked as Victoria walked them to the door.

"I think Calvin went to pick up their daughter at college," Victoria said, then added, "He wasn't sure Elena should be driving after hearing what happened to Juniper."

Jack nodded and thanked her again before handing his card to her. "If you think of anything else that might help, give me a call."

"So, what do you think?" Jack asked Tassie as soon as they were outside.

"I thought it was weird that Victoria sidestepped your question instead of denying it when you asked her if she murdered Juniper."

"Yeah, I noticed that too." Jack frowned. "I'd like to check the video footage the *Cupcake Combat* people have and see if any of it shows someone put anything into Juniper's purse before talking to Ada."

Oh! That was a good idea. Hopefully, the murderer had slipped up and committed the crime on camera.

"Do you want some company?" she asked.

His mouth edged up. "If it's you and Baxter, of course. Unless you have to get back to Pupcakes."

CUPCAKES AND CORPSES 47

Tassie smiled. "Abby has it covered, so we're all yours."

Okay, perhaps that came out sounding a lot more forward than she intended. Unless it was one of those Freudian things? Then maybe it'd come out exactly the way she'd meant it.

Chapter 6

Bluewater Bay boasted quite a few Victorian homes similar to Junipers, and The Blueberry Blossom Bed and Breakfast was one of them. The B&B was much bigger than the other Victorians in town, of course, with three floors, a dozen guest rooms, and a huge, majestic turret. It was also beautifully located right on the coast, which made it a popular tourist destination all year round.

But their real claim to fame—as far as Tassie was concerned anyway—were their blueberry muffins. Sweet and moist and ginormous, they were too delicious for words. And best of all, you could get them to go even if you weren't a guest. That was because the Hibbards, the people who owned the bed and breakfast, loved the locals as much as they loved the tourists. The bed and breakfast had been in their family for five generations, and the current proprietors, Caroline and Myles, were proudly carrying on all the traditions of their parents, grandparents, and great-grandparents before them.

"I've never been to a bed and breakfast," Jack said, eyeing the Victorian with interest as they walked toward the building.

"You've never stayed in one?"

He shook his head. "Nah. I've never understood the obsession with them."

She laughed. "That's because you've never stayed in one. Staying at a great bed and breakfast is way better than a great hotel. It's cozier because it's more personal. The people who own them are all about individualized service and getting to know you. Plus, they know the area so they can tell you about all the hidden gems. And along with the bed, you get a yummy home-cooked breakfast."

He let out a deep chuckle. "Okay, you sold me on the idea." He held the door open for her and Baxter. "After you."

Once inside the homey, inviting entryway that led into the open common area, Jack headed straight for the front desk where Caroline was standing talking with Mayor Fillmore of all people, along with the Hibbards' Golden Retriever, Corn Dog, who wagged his tail at the sight of them. The redhead smiled and waved at Tassie and Baxter, curiosity on her face as her gaze alighted on Jack. While Jack had only moved to Bluewater Bay a few weeks ago, by now, everyone in the small town knew he was a detective.

Tassie waved back when she noticed the production crew from *Cupcake Combat* spread out in the chairs surrounding the unlit fireplace. Most of them were riveted by whatever they were looking at on their phones. She grabbed Jack's arm and pointed in that direction. Maybe if she and Jack were already deep in conversation with the *Cupcake Combat* people, the mayor wouldn't notice them.

No such luck.

"Detective!" the mayor called, hurrying over to them.

Jack stopped in mid-step, took a deep breath, then turned to face the man. "Mayor Fillmore."

The mayor straightened his shoulders, needing to look up at Jack because he was so much taller. "Chief Pennington told me that you're investigating Juniper Larabee's death as a murder. Why would you do that?"

Jack stared at the mayor like he'd asked why water wasn't wet. "Because it *is* murder."

Mayor Fillmore bristled. "How do you know?"

"Because there was refined peanut oil in Juniper's lip gloss," Jack said. "So, unless she put it in there herself, we can safely say she was murdered."

"We don't know that she didn't," Fillmore pointed out.

Jack scowled but didn't say anything. His look said it all.

"Okay, I see your point." The mayor sucked on his teeth, making his walrus mustache bob up and down. "Well, I don't like this."

Tassie fought the urge to snort. She was pretty sure Juniper probably liked it even less. The woman had just been murdered and Fillmore was worrying about how it affected him. So typical of him.

From where he stood beside Tassie's feet watching the exchange between Jack and the mayor with fascination, Baxter looked like he agreed with her.

"What about the town's reputation?" Fillmore demanded. "What about the *Cupcake Combat* show?!"

Jack clenched his jaw, clearly trying to keep a rein on his temper. "I think finding the person responsible for Juniper's murder is more important than a TV show right now. And I'm sure her family and friends feel the same."

That seemed to give the mayor pause—for all of thirty seconds.

"You know, we never had a murder in Bluewater Bay until you got here, Detective," Fillmore sneered.

"Well, excuse me for doing the job the town paid me to do," Jack shot back.

The mayor's mouth tightened as he pinned Jack with a glare. "I want this case closed quickly." He glanced at Tassie before glaring at Jack again. "And what is she doing here?"

"She's a consultant," Jack said without missing a beat.

The mayor frowned, then looked at Baxter. "And who is that? Her crime-fighting dog?" He held up a hand. "You know what? Never mind. I don't care. Just get this murder solved. Like yesterday."

"You didn't vote for him, did you?" Jack muttered as Fillmore walked away in a huff.

"Ugh. No," Tassie said, then grinned. "But he's not wrong about Baxter being a crime-fighting dog."

When Baxter smiled up at them happily, she and Jack both laughed.

The *Cupcake Combat* production crew—four men and two women—glanced up from their phones when she and Jack walked over. But not before Tassie saw what had them all so intrigued—Victoria's latest video telling the world that Juniper had been murdered.

Jack flashed his badge. "Detective Sterling, Bluewater Bay PD. And this is Tassie Drake, one of our consultants."

The dark-haired woman closest to Tassie grinned up at them as she reached out to pet Baxter. "And who is this little cutie?"

Tassie smiled. "This is Baxter."

"Hey there, Baxter," the woman greeted him as he wagged his tail.

"I'm Nathan," the blond guy with glasses sitting on the chair closest to the fireplace said, then pointed to the rest of the crew in turn, starting with the woman who'd pet Baxter. "That's Melissa, Amy, Randy, Steve, and Tim." After they all nodded and/or waved, Nathan added, "Is this about that woman who was murdered?"

"It is," Jack said. "We were hoping we could get a look at your video footage from the taping yesterday. See if there's anything that might help us figure out who killed her."

Nathan sat up, his face eager. Everyone else seemed just as excited to help.

"Yeah. Sure," Nathan said. "I can show you on my laptop. We've got tons of footage." He glanced at Jack as he tapped on the keys. "What are you looking for?"

"Right now, we're just looking for anything suspicious," Jack told them noncommittally.

Tassie picked Baxter up as Nathan located the video so her pup could watch it too. Melissa, Amy, Randy, Steve, and Tim all crowded around, some of them sitting on the area rug as they reviewed the footage. As a huge fan of *Cupcake Combat*, it was fun looking at the raw, unedited footage. They'd started filming before the show even began taping, taking in the crowd as people arrived and took their seats, as well as the judges' table on the dais.

Juniper had her sleek, designer purse with her before the show started, then handed it off to Victoria, who placed it on her chair alongside her own oversized hobo bag. A minute later, Juniper called Victoria back up to the dais. Victoria hurried up to do her bidding, but not before saying something to Ada, who was sitting beside her digging in her own handbag, like she was looking for something.

Tassie leaned a little closer as Ada glanced over her shoulder, then picked up Juniper's purse and set it on her lap. She stuck her hand inside and rooted around.

"Do you think she's putting something in there?" Tassie asked Jack.

He frowned. "It's difficult to tell from this angle."

"But her hand is closed, like she has something in it," Tassie pointed out.

"Agreed."

A few moments later, Ada set Juniper's bag on Victoria's seat again, then stood up, turning away from the camera a little. A little while after that, the show started.

Jack wanted to watch the video all the way through to the part where Juniper went into anaphylactic shock but, thankfully, he wanted to see the view from the camera trained on the audience to see Victoria's and Ada's reactions. The shock on both of their faces appeared genuine, but it was possible that they were simply good actors.

"Did any of you overhear the contestants talking about Juniper?" Tassie asked.

"Irene and Gwen seemed more interested in beating each other than in Juniper," Nathan said.

Melissa nodded. "He's right. I did hear Hazel and her assistant talking about Juniper though. Charlotte was really concerned because Juniper hated Hazel and was sure there was no way she could win. Hazel definitely seemed nervous but said that Juniper had already taken so much from her and that she wasn't going to take the title of *Cupcake Combat* Champion from her too."

That sounded like motive to Tassie. She exchanged looks with Baxter and then Jack to see that they both seemed to be thinking the same thing.

"Thanks for the help," Jack told the crew.

"Sure thing," Nathan said. "If you need to see the footage again or anything, let us know. We'll be hanging around here until the boss tells us if we're going to do the show or pack it in and head to the next location."

"Is that a possibility?" Tassie asked.

The guy shrugged. "Depends on the network, but yeah."

"Mayor Fillmore won't be happy about that," Tassie muttered to Jack as they turned to see the man himself eyeing them from over by the door leading to the back deck where he was speaking with Pierre and Mia, the stars of *Cupcake Combat*.

Seeing that she and Jack were finished looking at the video, the mayor said something to the pair, then hurriedly headed their way.

"Detective, a word." Fillmore threw her and Baxter a pointed glare. "Alone."

Jack gave Tassie a look that was a mix of apologetic and annoyed.

She pointed at the front desk. "We'll wait over there."

Caroline graced her and Baxter with a welcoming smile as Corn Dog came over to greet them both. The redhead glanced over at Jack and the mayor.

"Is that about what happened to Juniper?" Caroline asked.

Tassie sighed. "Probably."

More likely, the mayor had heard about The Dessert Channel changing their mind about filming in Bluewater Bay and wanted to stress how important quickly closing this investigation was. But she didn't say that.

"Do the police know who did it?" Caroline asked. "Was it Hazel?"

Tassie glanced down at Baxter and Corn Dog to see them wagging their tails and booping each other's noses.

"The police aren't sure yet," Tassie said.

Neither was she. Of course, they'd only talked to Victoria so far, and Ada was a definite suspect. But as Tassie had learned from the previous murder she'd solved, there always seemed to be more suspects.

"Well, my money is on Hazel," Caroline said.

"Really?" Tassie asked. "Why do you think she did it?"

Caroline shrugged, leaning over to caress Corn Dog's fur. "It just seems kind of obvious, I guess. Juniper made a video talking about all the bakers competing on *Cupcake Combat* and really dissed Hazel. She said that Hazel was a pity entry, that she didn't deserve to be on the show because there was no way a home baker like her could compete with two experienced pastry chefs like Gwen and Irene, much less win *Cupcake Combat*."

Tassie cringed. "Ouch."

"I know, right?"

"Any idea why Juniper didn't like Hazel?"

Caroline rolled her eyes. "Apparently, Juniper's husband, Calvin, and Hazel were high school sweethearts, and after graduation, Juniper stole him. The two have hated each other ever since."

Huh. That was interesting. And certainly a motive for murder. But that would mean Hazel's reaction to Juniper going into anaphylactic shock after eating the cupcake she'd made had all been an act. It had seemed so genuine, too.

Before Tassie could ask Caroline anything else, Jack walked up. From the set of his jaw, it looked like his conversation with Mayor Fillmore hadn't gone well.

"Fillmore wants to talk to the chief and me, so I have to go back to the station. He's in a huff that this murder investigation is putting Bluewater Bay on the map for the all the wrong reasons," Jack said. "We'll have to talk to Ada later."

"I could talk to her," Tassie offered.

Jack opened his mouth, presumably to tell her that was a good idea—because it was—but Caroline interrupted him.

"Ada isn't at school today. She took her senior culinary class to Bangor. She has a friend who's a pastry chef at a fancy French restaurant there and the woman is going to teach them how to make the perfect macarons," Caroline said, then added, "I know because Phoebe is in her class."

Phoebe was Caroline and Myles' teenage daughter.

"Well, that saves me a trip to the high school then. Thanks." Tassie smiled. "Hopefully, she'll bring some macarons home to you and Myles."

Caroline grinned. "Fingers crossed."

It would have been cool if Ada had taken them to Bangor to make macarons when she was in high school, Tassie thought. She loved macarons.

"It's a little odd that Ada is at work today, don't you think?" Tassie asked as they left the bed and breakfast. "She and Juniper were supposed to be best friends."

Jack shrugged. "Maybe she didn't want to send her class to Bangor with a substitute."

"Maybe. Though Ada might not even be our main suspect," Tassie said as Jack slowed his SUV to a stop in front of Pupcakes a few minutes later. "It could be Hazel." She quickly filled him in on the vitriolic video Juniper had made about the home baker right before *Cupcake Combat*. "Baxter and I are going to talk to her."

"Good idea," Jack said. "But be careful. If she says anything that makes you think she's the murderer, get out of there."

"I will," she promised. "I'll call if I learn anything interesting."

He flashed her a grin. "You can call even if you don't."

Chapter 7

After Jack dropped them off, Tassie went into Pupcakes so Baxter could get some water, and she could fill her sister in on everything. Not that there was much to tell yet when it came to the investigation, but she knew Abby would be interested anyway. Plus, she wanted to make sure Abby was cool with minding the bakery while she and Baxter played amateur detective for the rest of the day.

As Tassie expected, Abby didn't mind at all. She was great like that.

Hazel lived in a small New England cottage that had a charming covered front porch with two rocking chairs painted the same forest green color as the home's shutters, as well as flowers in the front that were just starting to bloom. Tassie stepped onto the porch, Baxter at her side, and tapped the door knocker. Shaped like a small Nantucket basket filled with flowers, it was as adorable as the rest of the house.

Hazel opened the door a few moments later.

Tassie smiled. "I'm Tassie Drake. We met yesterday at the *Cupcake Combat* taping."

Hazel returned her smile with a nod. "Of course! I remember you. And this little cutie." She bent to give Baxter a pet before straightening up. "Come in."

The cottage was lovely on the inside, the entryway leading into a living room with hardwood floors, exposed beams on the ceiling, and a comfortable-looking couch and pair of wingback chairs. On the opposite side of the room, a staircase led up to the second floor.

But it was the kitchen that was the real focal point of the downstairs. While it wasn't as big or as grand as the kitchen in Juniper's guest house, it was still a baker's dream. The completely white kitchen had a fantastic double oven and colorful accents everywhere, including the vintage turquoise fridge and matching stand mixer on the butcher block island. Shadow boxes with all the blue ribbons Hazel had won at various competitions decorated the walls, a reminder of the excellent baker she was.

"Something smells yummy," Tassie said as Hazel led the way to the kitchen table.

Hazel laughed. "Thank you! I just baked a batch of peanut butter stuffed brownies. They're still cooling, otherwise, I'd offer you one."

Tassie smiled even though she was a little bummed. She'd never had a peanut butter filled brownie, but as they combined two of her favorite things, she knew she'd love them. "I definitely wouldn't turn it down if you did, but I understand. I'll just settle for enjoying the delicious scent of chocolate and peanut butter."

Apparently, so did Baxter. Her fur baby was sniffing the air appreciatively. He was well aware he couldn't eat chocolate, but he knew that almost all of the doggy treats she and Abby baked were made with peanut butter—and he loved the stuff. She didn't blame him.

"Would you like a cup of tea or some coffee?" Hazel asked. "Maybe something cold to drink?"

"I'm fine, thanks," Tassie said. "I wanted to come by and check to see how you're doing after what happened yesterday."

Hazel gave her a grateful look. "That's so sweet of you. I admit that I was shaken up yesterday—especially when I thought my cupcake killed Juniper—but after the statement that Chief Pennington put out saying she wasn't murdered by something I made, I feel much better." She paused, frowning. "Not that I'm relieved Juniper was murdered. I just meant..."

"It's okay. I know what you meant." Tassie offered her a small smile. "Did you know Juniper well?"

"We went to high school together."

Tassie feigned surprise. "You were friends then."

"We used to be."

Tassie *knew* there was a story behind Juniper's video. Not that it made Hazel a murderer, of course. She refused to have any preconceived notions here. Still, she couldn't wait to find out what happened between the two women. Especially after what Melissa from the *Cupcake Combat* crew said she overheard.

"Oh?" she said.

Hazel let out a sigh. "Calvin—Juniper's husband—and I were high school sweethearts. We even talked about getting married after college."

That all tracked with what Caroline said. But Tassie couldn't let Hazel know that she knew.

"What happened?" she asked.

Hazel made a face. "Juniper happened. I thought she was my friend, but she always wanted Cal for herself and would do anything to get him, including going to the same college that he did." Her mouth tightened. "He broke up with me his freshman year and married Juniper that summer. It's kind of ironic really. Juniper and I competed in every baking contest from the time we were kids, and I always came in first place, but she ended up winning the heart of the man I loved."

Okay, Tassie hadn't expected that. But if Juniper stole Hazel's boyfriend, what in the world did she have to be angry about? If anything, Hazel had way more right to be furious with her.

But was Hazel mad enough to kill her?

"That's awful," Tassie said. "I'm sorry."

Hazel nodded, blinking back tears. Even though it had been decades ago, it was obvious the pain was still fresh for her.

"It must have been difficult seeing them around town," Tassie said.

"It was," Hazel admitted, then shook her head. "It got worse when Juniper started her stupid channel and turned into an internet sensation. I don't know how it was possible, but she was even more insufferable and full of herself."

Since she hadn't known Juniper, Tassie would have to take Hazel's word for it. But from what she'd seen at the *Cupcake Combat* taping, Juniper did like being the center of attention.

"Were you also friends with Ada?" Tassie asked.

"I was," Hazel said. "Until she decided to be Juniper's maid of honor at her wedding. Not that I was surprised. Juniper comes from money and Ada always liked being around wealth. I think she thought it would rub off on her."

Hmm. Tassie hadn't realized Juniper came from a rich family. That explained the expensive Victorian home up on the cliffs.

The whole old money thing gave Tassie an idea though.

"Do you think Calvin married Juniper because she had money?"

Hazel shook her head without even having to think about it. "Definitely not. Calvin never cared about money."

Or maybe he cared about it more than Hazel thought.

"Do you know who might have wanted to kill Juniper?"

Hazel snorted. "Twenty-five years ago, I would have been at the top of the list. Back when she stole Calvin from me, I did want to kill her."

Sitting on the floor beside her chair, Baxter perked his ears, keenly interested in where this was going. Tassie was curious, too. Not that she expected Hazel to confess or anything. She'd learned from her first foray into solving a murder that killers didn't usually confess. Nope. They made you work for it.

"And what about now?"

Hazel hesitated, making Tassie wonder what she was thinking. Was she surprised by the question? She shouldn't be, considering she'd kind of walked right into it with that comment about wanting to kill Juniper all those years ago. Or maybe she was simply choosing her words carefully.

After a moment, Hazel sighed. "I'm over what Juniper did to me. It was a long time ago and I'm too old for nonsense like this, even if she wasn't."

"You're talking about the video she made about you competing in *Cupcake Combat*," Tassie said.

Hazel nodded. "There was no need for her to do that. It was petty. And so typical of her."

Tassie exchanged looks with Baxter. Hazel might think she was over Juniper's betrayal, but from everything she was saying, it didn't seem that way.

"It must have been stressful competing in a baking contest where Juniper would get to help pick the winner," Tassie observed. "With the rift between you, it's difficult to imagine she would have wanted you to win."

"I'm sure she wouldn't have." Hazel gave her an apologetic smile and motioned toward the counter. "I'm sorry. My niece is getting married and I'm making the wedding cake so she's coming over in a few minutes to talk about the design. Let me give you some of those peanut butter stuffed brownies to take with you."

As dismissals went, it wasn't the worst. And Hazel *was* giving her brownies in addition to all that information she'd spilled.

Both of which Tassie could share with Jack when she stopped by the station.

Chapter 8

Hazel had put the brownies in a bakery-style box with a cute foil sticker on top with the name of her blog, so the goodies transported well from her place back into town. Tassie realized she probably should have texted Jack to check to see if he was at the station before surprising him, but before she could even ask Lucy if he was there, her friend grinned and jerked her thumb toward his office.

"Jack's in there," she said.

Tassie led Baxter to a stop in front of Lucy's desk. "This newfound ability you have to read my mind is kind of weird."

Lucy's smile broadened. "I don't have to be a mind reader to know you like Jack."

Tassie quickly looked around. There was no one else in the bullpen at the moment, but the doors to both Jack's and Chief Pennington's offices were open, and there was a uniformed officer at the front desk. "Can you say that a little louder? I don't think they heard you down at the dog park."

Her friend waved a hand, making a dismissive sound.

Tassie opened the box of brownies and held it out. "Here. If you're eating one of these, you won't be blabbing about my love life."

Although it was probably better to let everyone think she was visiting Jack solely because she liked him instead of helping him with a murder investigation. While Mayor Fillmore might not care that she was a *consultant*, Chief Pennington could be a completely different story.

Lucy leaned forward to peek in the box. "Ooh, brownies."

"Peanut butter stuffed brownies," Tassie said. "Compliments of Hazel."

Her friend glanced up as she took a brownie and placed it on a paper napkin she got from her desk drawer before handing Tassie a few, presumably for her and Jack. "How's she doing?"

"She's happy that her cupcake didn't kill Juniper."

"I'll bet," Lucy said, taking a bite of brownie. "Oh! This is good!"

Tassie laughed. "We're going to leave you two alone and go see Jack."

Baxter pranced happily beside her as they walked through the bullpen to Jack's office. He looked up as she knocked lightly on the open door.

Jack flashed her a grin. "Hey! Come in."

Tassie slipped into one of the chairs in front of his desk, unhooking Baxter's leash from his harness so he could roam around the office. He immediately walked around to greet Jack.

"How did your meeting go with the mayor?" she asked.

Jack snorted. "About as well as you'd expect. Fillmore chewed my ear off about solving Juniper's murder in record time so that The Dessert Channel can tape *Cupcake Combat*. He heard that they're thinking of taking Bluewater Bay off their schedule entirely and flipped out."

Tassie groaned. "I was afraid he'd find that out."

"Well, the good news is that I think I was able to talk him off the ledge while still informing him that I intend to do a thorough investigation *Cupcake Combat* or no *Cupcake Combat*."

She would have loved to have seen the mayor's face when Jack told him that.

"Speaking of which, my conversation with Hazel was very interesting," she said, filling him on everything the woman had told her. "I didn't get a murderer vibe from her, but Melissa did overhear her say she was determined to make sure Juniper didn't take anything else from her so Baxter and I are keeping her on our list of suspects because she still had motive."

Jack's mouth twitched as he leaned his chair back. "You and Baxter have your own list of suspects?"

She nodded. "Of course. That way we can compare our list to yours and come up with the killer."

"I don't keep a list."

She frowned. "You don't."

"Nope."

"Then how do you keep track of all the suspects?"

"I write everything down in my notebook."

Yup, he did do that. "Oh. If you don't keep a list, then I suppose you don't make a murder board. You know. Like they do in all the TV shows."

"Afraid not."

"Well, that's...a bummer. I think they're kind of cool."

He chuckled. "Well, if you want to make a murder board, we definitely can."

She nodded, considering that before changing the subject. "Can you get a look at Juniper's will so we can see if she left anything to Ada? If Hazel is right about her being all about the money, that could be motive."

"I've already got something set up to see the judge about a warrant for that."

She smiled. "Great minds think alike."

"And so do ours," he teased.

Tassie couldn't help laughing at his joke even as her gaze settled on the bakery box in her lap. "I almost forgot! Hazel gave me some brownies. Peanut butter stuffed brownies, to be exact."

Jack sat up in his chair, face eager and hungry as she handed him one of the napkins Lucy had given her, then opened the box and offered him his pick. "Two of my favorite foods in one."

"Mine, too!" she said. "It took a lot of willpower not to eat one of these on the way over here."

The only real thing that stopped her was knowing she'd probably get peanut butter and chocolate everywhere and show up at Jack's office looking like she'd gotten into a fight with a Reese's Peanut Butter Cup and lost.

"I never had a suspect give me brownies," he remarked.

"That's because when you talk with someone, they automatically think you consider them a suspect," she said brightly. "They don't think that when they talk to me."

He grunted. "Good point."

After he chose a brownie, she helped herself to one of the decadent squares. Baxter left his position by the window where he'd been looking out to sit by her chair, his nose working overtime at all the yumminess filling the air even though he knew dogs couldn't eat chocolate.

"Oh, wow!" she practically moaned after taking a careful nibble so none of it ended up on her clothes. The sweetness of the chocolate combined with the salty peanut butter came together to create the most perfect brownie she'd ever tasted. "These are delicious!"

On the other side of the desk, Jack was clearly enjoying the chocolatey treat as much as she was. "If the cupcakes Hazel makes for *Cupcake Combat* are even half as amazing as this, then she's winning that competition hands-down. Well, providing she didn't murder Juniper and isn't in jail."

Good point.

"I think you're right." Tassie savored another taste of chocolate and peanut butter. "It must stink being allergic to peanuts."

Jack finished his brownie, then wiped his hands on the napkin. "I don't even want to think about that. Next to chocolate, peanut butter is the best thing ever. In fact, PB&J might just be the most perfect sandwich ever created."

He wasn't wrong.

"What kind of jelly do you go with?" Tassie asked.

"Strawberry preserves all the way," Jack said without hesitation.

"Me, too! I know everyone seems to like grape, but I'm all about strawberry."

"I think you're the first person to ever agree with me on that." His mouth curved. "Now, I'll have to be sure to bring some peanut butter and jelly sandwiches the next time we meet up at the dog park."

A little flutter went through her. Even though they hadn't been on an official "date" yet, it was still fun discovering all the stuff they had in common. Like the fact that neither of them liked seafood. That was almost a criminal offense to most people when you lived in a seaside town in Maine.

Tassie finished her brownie, then wiped her fingers on the napkin. Seeing that she was done eating, Baxter deftly jumped onto her lap. She rested her hands on either side of him.

"I can't help thinking that what happened with Hazel and Juniper back in high school is similar to this mess with Gwen and Irene," she mused.

"Did they both like the same guy in high school or something?" Jack asked.

Tassie shook her head, caressing Baxter's fur. "No, but there *is* a guy caught up in all the drama. Irene's brother, Graham, has been in love with Gwen since we were in high school but was always too shy to make a move. Now, he wants to ask her out but doesn't want to hurt Irene."

Jack seemed to consider that but didn't say anything right away. "You know I have to question your friends about Juniper's murder, right?"

Um, no, she hadn't known that. Which, in retrospect, was kind of silly. Everyone involved in *Cupcake Combat* was probably a suspect.

"You don't honestly think either of them killed Juniper, do you?" Tassie asked.

She'd already helped prove one friend innocent. Now, she might have to do the same for Gwen and Irene. Because she was sure neither of them murdered Juniper.

"I don't," Jack said. "But you saw how many people were moving around the park yesterday. Anyone could have slipped the tampered items in Juniper's purse."

Which meant the murderer might be someone they hadn't considered. Because as Jack said, there were a *lot* of people milling around the park. Of course, that would only make solving Juniper's murder trickier.

Jack looked like he wanted to say more, but his cell phone rang, interrupting him. He picked it up from the desk where he'd left it and thumbed the green button. "Detective Sterling," he said, then listened a moment. "I'll be right there." He hung up and looked at her. "The judge is ready to see me about that warrant for Juniper's will. Talk later?"

"Yeah, of course."

Tassie hooked Baxter's leash to his harness and stood, setting him on the floor, then picked up the box with the brownie for Abby.

"I'll walk out with you," Jack said, falling into step beside her.

She smiled and waved to Lucy as they crossed the bullpen and headed for the door.

"Have I mentioned that you're a natural at this detective stuff?" Jack asked as they stepped outside. "I might just have to recruit you full-time."

Tassie laughed. "I appreciate the compliment, but I don't know if I could ever take you up on that because I love running Pupcakes. However, if I did, the deal has to include Baxter. He's the real brains of the outfit."

Prancing along beside her, Baxter grinned up at them in agreement, making her and Jack both laugh before they parted to go their respective ways, her and Baxter to Pupcakes, and him to get the warrant to get a look at Juniper's will. If they were lucky, maybe it'd point them toward the woman's killer.

Chapter 9

Abby was leaning over drawing on a sketchpad at the checkout counter in the back of the shop when Tassie and Baxter walked into Pupcakes. Her sister glanced up as the little bell above the door tinkled, smiling at the sight of her.

"I'm glad you're back," Abby said. "Come look at this."

The minute Tassie took off Baxter's harness, he went to hang out with Finn, the two of them heading for the breakroom and their toys and water bowls. She walked past the long rustic-looking table with its plethora of three-tiered stands piled high with a variety of homemade dog treats, eager to see what Abby had to show her.

"What do you think?" Abby asked when she walked around the counter to stand beside her.

Tassie took one look at the sketchpad and squealed. "Our booth for Dog Days! I love it!"

Dog Days was a festival held at the park in the summer where Bluewater Bay's dog lovers came together with their pups for a day of fun in the sun. There were games and food and contests, and even a photographer to take pictures of the fur babies and their parents, all for a donation to the town's no-kill animal shelter. As far as Tassie was concerned it was *the* event of the summer. They'd gone to Dog Days ever since they opened Pupcakes and always redesigned the previous year's booth to keep it fresh.

The design her sister had come up with featured adorable cartoon canines that looked a lot like Baxter and Finn. It was perfect! Abby had made it colorful and fun and completely captured the vibe of their doggy bakery.

"Did I tell you that Isaac is renting the booth next to ours?" Abby asked, leaning her hip against the counter and looking like the cat that licked the cream.

Isaac Bridger was a well-known dog psychologist new to Bluewater Bay who Abby was dating. Of course, instead of simply bumping into him at the coffee shop and starting up a conversation, her sister had pretended that Finn needed help with behavioral issues, which he didn't—something Isaac figured out right from their very first meeting. Luckily, Isaac hadn't been put off by the subterfuge and found Abby's shyness endearing.

Just more proof that he was a keeper.

"You and Isaac are getting close," Tassie observed as Baxter and Finn pranced out from the breakroom to see what they were up to. She bent to give each of them a pat even as her sister did the same.

"We are." Abby straightened, twirling her hair around her finger absently. "I really like him, Tassie."

Tassie couldn't help smiling. That much was obvious. "Yeah, I kind of figured as much since you guys practically spend all your free time together."

Her sister laughed but didn't say anything. A moment later, a frown furrowed her brow.

Oh, no. Tassie could sense a *but* coming.

"What is it?" she asked.

"Nothing. It's just that…" She hesitated like she was struggling with whether she should give voice to whatever was going on in her head. "I know things with Isaac are fantastic right now, but I can't help waiting for the other shoe to drop."

It was Tassie's turn to frown. "What are you talking about?"

Abby let out a sigh. "Every time I'm dating a guy who I think is perfect, I discover he's hiding something from me that I just can't get past. Like when Darren only pretended to like dogs because he wanted to go out with me."

At their feet, Baxter and Finn both made faces.

Tassie made one too. Yeah, Darren was a jerk. There was no getting around that. "Well, since Isaac is a dog psychologist, I don't think you have to worry about that."

Abby went on like she hadn't even heard a thing Tassie said. "Or when Eugene lied about having a great job and instead spent his days playing video games in his mother's garage."

Tassie had forgotten about Eugene. If you couldn't trust a guy to be honest with you about something as simple as what he did for work, what could you trust him to be honest about? Well, unless he was a spy or something, she supposed. "You already know Isaac isn't lying about what he does for a living."

Her sister chewed on her lip. "But what if he has some other deep, dark secret he's hiding?"

Tassie reached out and took her sister's hands in both of hers. "Abby, you're worrying over nothing. Isaac is a great guy who's already half in love with you."

At least, she *hoped* Isaac was a great guy. Her sister deserved to be happy, especially after the string of dopes she'd dated. And Isaac seemed like he checked all the boxes.

Then again, Tassie wasn't sure she was the best person to give advice on the subject. The last two guys she'd dated before Jack—well, *technically*, she and Jack weren't together yet—had been disasters. One had cheated on her and the other had been attracted to her because he felt she looked like a younger version of his mother. That still gave her the creeps every time she thought about it.

Abby considered her words for a long moment, then bobbed her head up and down. "You're right. I'm being silly." She smiled. "Speaking of great guys, how's Jack?"

Tassie grinned. "He's fine. We spent the morning doing some investigating then bonded over our love of peanut butter." She opened the bakery box and held it out to her sister. "Which reminds me! I went to talk to Hazel and she gave me some brownies. I saved you one."

Abby's eyes lit up as she took a taste. "Oh, yummy! Did I ever tell you that you're my favorite sister?"

"I'm your only sister," Tassie said dryly.

"That doesn't mean you aren't my favorite."

Sitting on the floor beside Tassie, Baxter clearly thought Abby was hilarious if the expression on his face was any indication. It *was* kind of funny. Before Tassie could say anything, both of their cell phones dinged. She dug hers out of her crossbody bag while Abby glanced over to check her cell where it sat on the counter.

It was a group text from their mom reminding them about coming to dinner that Friday.

How could they forget?

Drats.

That came out wrong. Thankfully, she hadn't actually said it aloud.

Tassie loved going to their parents' house and spending time with them, but having dinner with their mom and dad on that particular date wasn't a joyous event because it was their older brother's birthday. Ten years older than she was, Nolan had left home when he was eighteen and they hadn't seen or heard from him since. That had been almost twenty years ago. They had no idea if Nolan was even alive.

The worst part was that their mom and dad wouldn't tell them why Nolan left, much less mention his name. And yet, their mother always made his favorite meal for dinner followed by his favorite dessert, celebrating a birthday for a son and a brother they refused to talk about.

It was all very weird.

"What do you think of asking Mom and Dad about what happened with Nolan?" Tassie asked her sister.

"Again?" Abby frowned. "I don't know. Last time we tried it, Mom got really upset."

Tassie remembered and still felt awful about it. But in her defense, Nolan was her brother and she missed him. Not knowing why he'd left and what had happened to make him abandon his family, hurt.

Had he committed a crime and gone on the run so he wouldn't go to jail?

Had he gotten in a fight with their parents that was so ugly that he didn't want to be part of their family anymore?

Had he eloped with a girlfriend Tassie never knew he had because their mom and dad didn't approve of her?

The possibilities were myriad.

As if sensing her distress, Baxter rubbed up against her leg. Tassie reached down to pet him.

"Abby, don't you want to know why Nolan left?" she asked.

Her sister sighed. "You know I do."

"Then let's talk to Mom and Dad, and this time, we'll refuse to stop asking what happened with our brother until we get an answer."

Chapter 10

Drats.

"We're out of cinnamon chai tea," Tassie announced the next morning, walking out of the breakroom and into the main part of Pupcakes, Baxter prancing along beside her. She'd have to remember to put some on the shopping list. Not to be confused with her murder suspect list. "I'm going to run over to Hug in a Mug and grab some. Do you want anything?"

Abby looked up from the computer at the counter where she was doing inventory. "I'll take an iced green tea."

Hmm. A cold drink actually sounded good. *Maybe I should get an iced cinnamon chai instead,* Tassie thought as she slipped Baxter's harness on and attached his leash.

Even though there was never a lot of traffic in Bluewater Bay, Tassie looked both ways before she and Baxter crossed the street to the coffee shop. At the counter,

Aria was making fresh coffee and she glanced over her shoulder as they walked in.

"Hey!" she said, finishing up and turning around. "What can I get for you guys?"

Tassie smiled. "One iced cinnamon chai tea and one iced green tea."

"Coming right up!"

While she waited, Tassie glanced around the coffee shop. A handful of people sat at the cozy tables, some of them on their laptops, others reading books. A girl of about twenty sat at the farthest table, focused on her cell phone. Dark-haired, she wore glasses, sneakers, leggings, and a hoodie with the name *Bay Shore College* emblazoned across the front.

Tassie started to turn back to the counter when she realized that the girl looked familiar. Taking out her phone, she did a quick Google search to check and realized she was right.

It *was* Elena Larabee.

Juniper's daughter.

Knowing she probably wouldn't get a better opportunity to talk to the girl, Tassie quickly paid for the teas and thanked Aria.

Jack had called last night to say he got the warrant for Juniper's will and would be meeting with her lawyer this morning, so Tassie had plenty of time to do some investigating with Baxter on their own before they went over to the high school that afternoon to talk to Ada after the woman was done with classes for the day.

With that in mind, she picked up the tray of drinks, then walked over to Elena's table.

"Elena?" she said.

The girl looked up, dark eyes curious.

"I'm Tassie Drake. I own Pupcakes, the doggy bakery across the street," she said. "And this is Baxter."

When Elena smiled at both of them, Tassie took that as an invitation to slip into the chair across from the girl.

"I just wanted to tell you how sorry I was to hear about your mother," Tassie said.

Elena nodded, her smile fading. "Thank you. Did you know my mother well?"

"Just from her YouTube Channel."

Okay, that was a little bit of a fib. She *did* know Juniper from her YouTube Channel. She'd simply never watched Juniper's videos. But Elena didn't need to know that.

"Her YouTube Channel." On the other side of the table, Elena made a face. "Of course."

From where he was sitting beside her chair, Baxter gave Tassie a pointed look, obviously picking up on the underlying resentment in Elena's voice.

"You didn't like that she had a YouTube Channel?" Tassie asked.

Elena stared at her cup, absently rubbing her thumb over the Hug in a Mug logo printed on it like she was trying to decide how to answer that question.

"I thought it was cool in the beginning," she finally said. "I was in high school then and she'd film in our kitchen, getting real about being extremely allergic to peanuts and everything made with them. She'd share recipes and offer tips and become friends with other people who were dealing with the same allergy." Her lips curved a little, her gaze taking on a faraway look. "She was so nervous making those first videos and I was so proud of her for doing it."

"What changed?"

Elena let out a snort, her voice bitter when she spoke. "She became an internet sensation and stopped being my mother."

Tassie frowned. "What do you mean?"

"I mean the *only* thing she cared about was that stupid channel and being an influencer. She didn't care that it interfered with everyone else's life."

"By *everyone else's*, you mean yours?"

"Yeah. And my dad's." Elena sipped her coffee. "I know she was trying to build her brand and everything, and at first it was kind of cool having a mom who was so hip about the whole social media thing. But before long, the brand became her life. For all intents and purposes, I lost my mother."

"It couldn't really have been that bad, could it?" Tassie asked.

This was merely a case of a girl barely out of her teens blowing everything out of proportion, right?

"It was that bad and worse," Elena muttered. "I went from having a mom who was always there for me to having one who was never there for anything. Not parent-teacher conferences, not my gymnastic meets, not my piano recitals, not the time I got dumped by my first boyfriend. She wasn't there on prom night to take pictures or at my high school graduation or any of the other half-dozen times she should have been because she was too busy being a celebrity. She couldn't even be bothered to drop me off at college my freshman year because she was too busy appearing on some morning TV show in Bangor that day. She missed everything and never even considered apologizing. I spent so much time over the last few years being furious at her, and now, she's gone." Her eyes shone with tears, and she reached up to wipe the wetness from her face. "I'm sorry."

"Don't be," Tassie said gently. "Your mother was just murdered, Elena."

She sniffed and nodded, clearly trying not to cry.

Tassie glanced at Baxter to see that he looked as uncomfortable as she was. Talking to a suspect who was so close to the murder victim was a decidedly uncomfortable experience. The other time she and Baxter had been down this road—in this very coffee shop, as a matter of fact—the guy hadn't been at all close to his father so treating him as a suspect had been easy. Sitting across from Elena and wondering if she murdered a mother she clearly cared about felt wrong.

But just because Elena cared about her mother, that didn't mean she *didn't* kill Juniper. Especially since there'd obviously been a whole boatload of resentment on Elena's part about Juniper ignoring her in the pursuit of building her brand and becoming an internet celebrity. Granted, tampering with Juniper's lip gloss and auto-injectors screamed pre-meditation, but Elena might have been angry enough at the time to plot her mother's murder when she tampered with the stuff, then regretted it later.

"When did you last see your mother?" Tassie asked.

"The day before *Cupcake Combat*." Elena glanced at her before staring into her coffee cup again. "My boyfriend and I were supposed to have dinner with my parents. It was the first time I was bringing him home to meet them. But it turned out that my mom couldn't come with us because she decided it was more important to have dinner with the people from that show instead. We had this huge fight and I... I said some terrible things. It was the last time I saw her." She shook her head. "I still can't believe she's gone."

Elena quickly picked up her cup, sipping her drink as she fought back more tears. Tassie gave her the time she needed, her heart going out to the girl. At her side, Baxter looked concerned, clearly sensing Elena's emotion, and Tassie reached down and gave him a comforting pat.

"Do you know anyone who might have wanted to kill your mother?" Tassie asked after a long moment.

Elena considered that, her brows knitting. "Mom never went out of her way to be nice to people, I guess, but I'm not sure who would have hated her enough to murder her. I mean, she fought with everyone—me, Dad, Victoria, Ada. You name it."

"What about Hazel?"

She sighed. "I know they didn't like each other and that it went all the way back to high school because they liked the same guy—my dad. Even though Dad picked Mom over Hazel, I think my mother still felt threatened by her. If Dad even said hello to Hazel when they passed each other on the street, Mom lost it."

"Wow."

"Yeah," Elena agreed. "In a way, I kind of felt sorry for Hazel."

"Because of what happened with your father?"

Especially since, to hear Hazel tell it, Juniper had stolen Calvin from her.

"No," Elena said. "For competing in an event where my mom had a vote in whether she won or not."

"Because Hazel would never win," Tassie said.

Elena nodded. "Pretty much."

Tassie exchanged looks with Baxter to see he obviously thought that was a motive for murder too. Maybe Hazel thought that with Juniper dead, the show would pick a new local celebrity judge who was more impartial. She probably wouldn't be wrong. It was hard to imagine a person would kill someone over the title of *Cupcake Combat* Champion, though. But when the two people in question had as much bad blood between them as Juniper and Hazel, perhaps it wasn't so far-fetched after all.

Chapter 11

Elena needed to go home to meet up with her boyfriend who was driving down from Bay Shore College to be with her, so Tassie walked out of Hug in a Mug with the tray of iced teas in one hand and Baxter's leash in the other.

Gwen was outside The Cupcakery setting up a sandwich board announcing the day's special cupcake—peach bourbon with peach buttercream—and she waved as Tassie and Baxter walked across the street. Today, she wore her signature cupcake pattern apron over a white top and a pair of khaki capri pants.

Tassie smiled while Baxter wagged his tail in greeting.

"Was that Juniper's daughter with you?" Gwen asked, her gaze curious as she followed the girl down the street.

"It was," Tassie said. "I was just telling her how sorry I was about Juniper."

Gwen nodded, understanding on her face as she bent to give Baxter a pat. "That was awful, wasn't it? I still can't believe what happened. Poor Juniper."

"Did you know Juniper well?" Tassie asked.

She wasn't asking because she suspected Gwen murdered her, of course. She was actually hoping Gwen might be able to give her some clue about who'd killed Juniper. Because while she might not consider Gwen a suspect, Jack almost certainly did. She didn't blame him. That *was* his job. But it meant that she needed to figure out who the real murderer was before he started arresting another one of her friends.

Gwen shrugged. "Juniper and I weren't friends, but I saw her around town and watched her videos sometimes. She couldn't eat any of the cupcakes I made because my bakery isn't peanut-free, so she never came into the shop."

Tassie remembered that Victoria had mentioned Ada and Juniper opening a peanut-free bakery. It would definitely be the only one in Bluewater Bay. Maybe they were more popular in big cities.

"Did you see Juniper talking to anyone before the competition?" she asked.

Gwen thought a moment. "She spent some time talking to Victoria and Ada, then made the rounds, stopping by each of our tables with Pierre and Mia to say hello. Mostly, she made a bunch of videos on her phone for her fans."

Yeah, Tassie noticed Juniper doing a lot of that too.

"The conversation between Juniper and Hazel must have been interesting," she remarked, then added, "I heard she said some rather unflattering things about Hazel on her channel."

Gwen grimaced. "Yeah, I saw that. Juniper said some pretty mean things about her that were really unwarranted. Saying that Hazel didn't deserve to be in the competition because she was a home baker and not classically trained, when she'd already won so many baking contests was hateful if you ask me."

Tassie silently agreed but it sounded like Juniper had still been jealous of Hazel and enjoyed sticking it to her every chance she got.

"Then again, Juniper didn't have very many nice things to say about me either," Gwen continued. "She claimed that a friend told her my cupcakes were dry and that I'd better fix that issue if I wanted to win *Cupcake Combat*."

"Your cupcakes aren't dry!" Tassie protested.

Gwen's lips curved. "Thanks. Luckily, my other customers agree with you. I think Juniper sometimes said things like that simply to get clicks. Although, she was spot on when she said Irene wouldn't be much competition for anyone since cupcakes aren't her thing."

That was unfair to say, and Gwen knew it. While it was true that Irene didn't have any of them on the menu at her bakery—mostly because everyone went to Gwen's for those—she still made a delicious cupcake when she did make them.

Tassie's first instinct was to tell Gwen that, but then she caught herself. Right now, she needed to focus on finding Juniper's killer. She'd figure out how to fix Gwen and Irene's friendship later.

"Did you happen to overhear what Juniper and Hazel talked about when she stopped by her kitchen?" she asked.

"Pierre and Mia did most of the talking when they got to Hazel's station," Gwen admitted. "Hazel spent more time talking to Victoria."

That was interesting.

"Are the two of them friends?" Tassie asked.

Gwen pursed her lips in thought before answering. "I don't know if they're friends, but I know Victoria went to school with Hazel's niece. I heard Hazel remind Victoria about her niece's bridal shower. She's getting married soon."

Tassie nodded. "Hazel mentioned something to me about making her niece's wedding cake. Did Hazel say anything to you about Juniper?"

"Not really. I was too focused on my own cupcakes. Though I did hear her sister, Charlotte, mention to Hazel that she wished someone else was the town's celebrity judge instead of Juniper because she didn't think there was any way they could possibly win."

"What did Hazel say?"

"I didn't hear." Gwen shrugged. "What could she say? There wasn't anything they could do about it."

Or had they?

CUPCAKES AND CORPSES 91

Even with the history between Juniper and Hazel, Tassie found it difficult to imagine that Hazel—and maybe her sister—murdered Juniper. She seemed like such a sweet woman. If she'd killed Juniper wouldn't she have more of a tell?

Tassie groaned silently. Maybe she was letting those deliciously decadent peanut butter stuffed brownies cloud her thinking here.

Gwen frowned. "The police don't think that Hazel killed Juniper, do they?"

That was a sticky question. Technically, Jack hadn't said one way or another, but Tassie was sure Hazel was on the list. Well, if he *kept* a list.

"I'm not sure," she said noncommittally.

Gwen folded her arms. "Well, if they're looking at anyone for Juniper's murder, it should be Irene."

Tassie did a double take. From where he sat on the sidewalk beside her, even Baxter eyed Gwen in disbelief.

"Irene?" she said. "You're not serious."

She supposed she shouldn't be surprised. Irene wasn't Gwen's favorite person. But trying to get her arrested for murder was kind of low.

"But I am," Gwen insisted. "In fact, I saw Irene at The Culinary Connoisseur's Pantry the other day buying cold-pressed peanut oil."

The Culinary Connoisseur's Pantry was a gourmet food store in town. While the name was a mouthful—no pun intended—Tassie had to admit it had lots of things you couldn't get at the regular grocery store. Like cold-pressed peanut oil for one.

"Irene owns a bakery, Gwen. Buying cold-pressed peanut oil doesn't mean she used it to murder Juniper. I'm sure you purchase it too."

"It also doesn't mean Irene didn't use it." Gwen lifted her chin. "Did you know she had coffee with Juniper at Hug in a Mug right before *Cupcake Combat*?"

"No, I didn't."

But then again, Tassie didn't keep tabs on Irene the way Gwen seemed to.

"Don't you think that's suspicious?" Gwen asked.

"Suspicious, how?"

"I don't know. Maybe Juniper promised to make sure Irene won *Cupcake Combat*, then changed her mind, and Irene killed her."

As motives went, it wasn't that out of the box, if it were anyone else but Irene. Sure, she wanted to win *Cupcake Combat*—probably more to say she beat Gwen than to be crowned champion—but that didn't make her any different than Gwen. *Could Irene's desire to have bragging rights push her so far over the edge that she'd commit murder?*

Tassie couldn't believe that.

She exchanged looks with Baxter to see that he seemed as frustrated as she was. Sighing, she turned back to Gwen.

"This feud between you and Irene is getting a little ridiculous." Tassie knew she said she wasn't going to try to play peacemaker today, but Gwen was making it necessary. "What happened between the two of you?"

Gwen looked away. "Stuff."

"Yeah, I figured that much. What kind of stuff?"

Blue eyes met Tassie's, an old hurt reflected there. "You should really ask Irene. It's her fault anyway."

Tassie opened her mouth to say more but Gwen continued.

"I have to get back inside. Those cupcakes aren't going to bake themselves." She gave Tassie a forced smile. "I'll see you later."

Tassie sighed as Gwen disappeared into The Cupcakery. She looked at Baxter.

"Well, I don't know about you, but that makes me even more curious about what happened back in high school."

Baxter gazed up at her, the look in his sweet brown eyes telling her that he was just as interested as she was.

Chapter 12

Jack arrived at Pupcakes a little before three that afternoon to pick up Tassie and Baxter so they could go talk to Ada. The moment he stepped inside the shop, Baxter pranced over to greet him, tail wagging double-time. Jack stopped to give him a scratch behind his ears.

"Hey there, boy."

Tassie smiled at the pair of them as she took out a tray of peanut butter doggy treats from the oven and set them on the rack to cool. There was nothing that made an already gorgeous guy even more attractive than loving animals.

"Someone's happy to see you," she said with a laugh as Finn hurried over to get pets, too.

Jack grinned. "Hopefully, they aren't the only one."

Tassie felt herself blush a little. "They aren't."

Over at the counter, Abby couldn't hide her smile as she finished ringing up Harry Weber's purchase. A retired optician who always had a smile on his face, the elderly man came into Pupcakes once a week to buy treats for his Schnauzer, Archie.

Thanking Abby, Harry turned to head for the door only to stop when he saw Jack. Smiling, Harry reached out to shake his hand.

"Detective, how are you today?"

Jack returned his smile. "I'm doing well. And you, Harry."

"I'm fine. Just stopped in to get my baby some treats. Any luck figuring out who murdered Juniper yet?"

"Not yet," Jack admitted. "But we have some leads."

Harry clapped him on the shoulder as he made his way to the door "You'll figure it out, I'm sure."

"Endearing yourself to the locals, I see," Tassie said with a smile after Harry had left and Jack had greeted her sister.

"What do you mean?" he asked.

Tassie came out of the kitchen area into the main part of the store. "Just that there's nothing people in a small town love more than someone knowing their name."

She'd been a little concerned how receptive the townspeople would be to Jack taking over for the previous detective who retired. Everyone had loved Henry and thought that the Bluewater Bay Police Department would promote from within, but instead they'd hired Jack. Even though he was extremely qualified for the job—and no, she wasn't being biased saying that—he was also from Albany, New York, and that made him an outsider. But the town had immediately welcomed him.

And now, she realized that was in part thanks to Jack's excellent people skills.

"Oh. That." He chuckled. "Well, I have parents and grandparents who taught me that it doesn't take a lot of effort to be nice to people."

"They sound very smart," she said.

"They are," he agreed with a grin. "You ready to go see Ada?"

"Yup. Let me just get Baxter's harness on and grab my purse."

While she did that, Jack picked out some dog treats for Gus, putting them in the clear plastic bag provided and closing it with a twist-tie before bringing them over to the counter for Abby to ring up. Her sister had the sketchbook with the design for their booth open beside the register, which she proudly showed to him.

"You're coming to Dog Days, right?" Abby asked.

Jack's gaze slid to Tassie, mouth edging up. "Yeah. If I'm not working, I'll bring Gus. And if I am on duty, I told him that I'd stop by and take lots of pictures for him."

Tassie laughed along with her sister. Not at Jack, of course, because that's exactly something she would do for Baxter. It made him even more endearing.

Slipping her crossbody bag over her head, she looked at her sister. "We should be back in an hour or so."

Abby waved a hand. "Take your time. Have fun."

Outside, Tassie started for her SUV. "I need to grab Baxter's carrier. I'll just be a minute."

"I picked one up at the pet store for him yesterday," Jack said. "It's already in the backseat."

Tassie looked at him in surprise. "You did?"

He shrugged. "Yeah. I figured it'd be easier since you and Baxter ride with me so much."

"Oh." He wasn't wrong. Great minds thought alike. "That was thoughtful of you."

He flashed her a grin. "I'm a thoughtful guy."

Tassie laughed. Yeah, she'd already figured that out about him.

"I got a look at Juniper's will," Jack said as he pulled onto the street and headed toward the high school. "Calvin gets most of her money. The rest of it gets distributed evenly between Elena, Victoria, and Ada. And there's a lot of it to go around."

Tassie wasn't surprised by any of that, though she'd have thought Juniper would have left more to Elena than Victoria and Ada. But it still gave all of them motive, especially if they knew she'd named them in her will.

"With all that money floating around, that means Gwen and Irene aren't at the top of the suspect list," Tassie remarked. "Hazel, either."

"Money isn't always the motive in murder cases," Jack pointed out.

"You're right." Tassie sighed. "Do you think it would help to figure out who bought cold-pressed peanut oil recently?"

He nodded as he turned into the parking lot for the high school. "I already checked with the gourmet food store in town. Gwen, Irene, and Hazel all bought cold-pressed peanut oil within the past week, along with a lot of other people. Unfortunately, whoever killed Juniper might very well have purchased the peanut oil online, and there's no way I'll be able to get a warrant to search for that without more evidence."

Tassie fought the urge to snort. She wouldn't be surprised if Gwen bought that bottle of cold-pressed peanut oil the same day she claimed to see Irene purchase hers. Tassie needed to talk to Irene to figure out what had happened between them, and soon.

Bluewater Bay High was a two-story brick building surrounded by clusters of trees and sporting a big sign in blue and gold with the school's name and mascot, a seahawk. There was a lot of land around it, too, which was great for the various sports. Not that Tassie played any sports when she was in school, but it was fun going to watch games.

"You went to school here, right?" Jack said as they walked toward the front doors. "So you know where Ada's classroom is?"

Tassie nodded. "Yup. It's right by the cafeteria and easy to find."

He looked around as they walked through the halls. Painted blue, white, and gold, the seahawk pride and school spirit was everywhere. *Clearly, things haven't changed much since I was at Bluewater Bay High*, Tassie thought with a smile as a group of teens walked by, eyeing them curiously.

"How many students go here?" Jack asked.

"About five hundred."

He lifted a brow. "Wow."

"You seem surprised."

"I am. I'm also trying to imagine going to a high school with that many people."

"How big was your high school?"

He grew up in Albany, so it couldn't have had less students than her small town.

"Eight thousand people."

It was her turn to be stunned. In her arms, Baxter looked just as amazed.

"You're kidding!" she said.

He chuckled. "Nope. My class had over two thousand people in it."

"Whoa. Your graduation ceremony must have taken forever."

That earned her another laugh. "You have no idea. It took three hours for me to get my diploma and then another two after that."

"Yikes," she said. "I think my whole graduation ceremony took an hour."

Tassie stopped outside a classroom with a collage of fun, colorful kitchen posters. One showed various spices while others had drawings of utensils, descriptions of cooking and baking techniques, lists of different types of cuisines, and even mouthwatering photos of foods like gourmet burgers and frosted cakes.

The door was open, so Tassie led the way into the room. Stainless steel counters lined both walls to either side of them, sinks along one and cooktops on the other, while all the ovens were on the opposite end of the room. Stainless steel workstations filled the center of the room, each of which had its own stand mixer. Things like pots, pans, and utensils were on the shelves, and there was also a pantry and walk-in fridge/freezer combo.

But while the set-up was fancy, Baxter was way more interested in the myriad smells. His little nose was going a mile a minute.

Ada was in her office located right inside the door and she looked up as they walked in. Colorful and vibrant, there were lots of plants and more posters covering the wall, most of them featuring food, but there were also some with famous quotes from famous chefs. A few inches shorter than Tassie, she had wavy, shoulder-length auburn hair and gray eyes. Giving them a smile, she took off her reading glasses and got to her feet.

"Tassie! What a nice surprise!" She gazed warmly at Baxter, who wagged his tail in greeting. "And who is this little guy?"

Tassie smiled. "This is Baxter."

"Hello there, Baxter."

"I'm astounded you remember me," Tassie said as Ada pet Baxter. "I only took one class with you."

Ada turned her smile on Tassie again. "I remember all my students." She glanced at Jack. "Detective. Now, I know you weren't in any of my classes. This must be about Juniper."

"It is," he said. "I wonder if you have a few minutes to talk?"

Her smile faded, her eyes filling with sadness. "Of course. Come in and sit down."

Ada had two chairs in her office, so Tassie slipped into one of them with Baxter while Jack took the other.

"We weren't sure you'd be at school today after what happened," he said, taking out his notebook. The one that he used instead of making lists.

Ada sighed as she sat down behind her desk. Her office was decorated with more culinary-themed posters, and she had one of those coffee makers on a small sideboard that used little individual cups.

"I thought about taking time off, but I had my senior class trip to Bangor yesterday that I couldn't miss," she explained. "I realized that being here was easier than being at home thinking about Juniper."

Tassie supposed that made sense. Perhaps that sense of normalcy helped her process what had happened to the other woman.

"Victoria told us that you and Juniper were close," Tassie said.

Ada nodded, her eyes misting with tears. "We were. We went to high school together." She gave them a sad smile. "We actually sat in this very classroom together learning how to make chocolate souffle. Juniper's ended up looking like a disaster, but it tasted delicious anyway."

She laughed a little at the memory, then reached for a tissue, using it to dab at the corners of her eyes. "I'm sorry. This is just all so difficult. Who would do this to poor Juniper?"

"That's what we're trying to figure out," Jack said. "Do you know if she had any enemies?"

Ada thought for a moment. "We all have enemies, I suppose. Of course, Juniper probably had more than most, with her online presence and all."

"We're actually looking for someone closer to home," Jack explained. "Someone in town who would have had access to her purse long enough to slip the tampered lip gloss and auto-injectors in it."

She shook her head. "Juniper and her lip gloss. She used a very specific brand, you know?"

That might help them narrow down suspects, Tassie thought. "Who else knew what brand she used?"

"Anyone who watched her videos. Juniper always posted GRWM videos."

Jack glanced at Tassie, probably to see if she knew what the acronym stood for. "GRWM?"

"It stands for Get Ready with Me," Tassie told him. "It's this trend on social media where people post videos of them getting ready for an event or something like that. They put on makeup and share beauty tips, talk about their outfits—things like that."

Jack looked at her like she was making it up. "You're kidding. People actually do that?"

She nodded. "All the time. It's a super popular hashtag."

Ada backed her up. "Tassie's right. It's all over the internet."

Jack shook his head like he was trying to wrap his mind around that for a minute. "So, anyone could have tampered with the lip gloss."

That was true. But not everyone would know what brand of auto-injector Juniper used, right?

Unless she mentioned that in her videos, too.

"What was her relationship with her husband like?" Jack asked.

Where he was sitting on Tassie's lap, Baxter perked his ears up, like he was interested in knowing the answer to that, too.

"Calvin?"

Jack scribbled something in his notebook. "They weren't having any marital problems that you know of then?"

Her brow furrowed. "You don't think Calvin killed her, do you?"

Ada seemed genuinely horrified at the thought. Although, honestly, Calvin was the most likely suspect. Wasn't that what they said when there was a murder on the mysteries she liked to watch? It was always the husband. Or wife, she supposed.

"We're just gathering information right now," Jack said smoothly.

Ada nodded. "I understand. But I really think you're barking up the wrong tree when it comes to Calvin. No offense, Baxter."

"What about Hazel?" Tassie asked.

"Hazel is another story," Ada muttered. "She's hated Juniper ever since Calvin broke up with her and married Juniper."

"From the video she put online about the *Cupcake Combat* contestants, it sounds like Juniper hated Hazel just as much," Tassie observed.

"You're not wrong there," Ada agreed. "Juniper could have a mean streak in her when she wanted to. She took every chance she got to stick it to Hazel. I told her it was beneath her, but she wouldn't listen to me." Ada looked at Jack. "Are you sure there wasn't any peanut oil in that cupcake Hazel made?"

"I'm sure," he said. "We took a look at the video footage the *Cupcake Combat* people have and noticed that you went into Juniper's purse right before the show started taping."

Ada frowned. "Surely, you don't think that I had something to do with her murder?"

He gave Ada what Tassie was coming to learn was his patented *detective* smile. "Just trying to figure out what you were doing in her purse."

"I got a piece of gum. Juniper and I have been going in each other's purses since high school." She took a deep breath. "Juniper was my friend, Detective."

Jack nodded and closed his notebook. "Thanks for the help."

Ada eyed him warily as she pushed back her chair and stood, like she was afraid Jack was going to put her in handcuffs and take her to jail right then. Tassie wasn't ready to say Ada topped her list yet, but she was certainly still on it. Even if she and Juniper were friends. And she *had* gone into Juniper's purse.

"I'm sorry that you and Juniper didn't get to open that peanut-free bakery like you both wanted to," Tassie said as she got to her feet, Baxter in her arms. "Victoria made it sound like a great idea."

Ada grimaced. "Unfortunately, Juniper didn't agree."

"Oh?" Tassie said.

"Teaching is my calling, but I've always dreamed of having my own bakery and thought opening one that was peanut-free was a fantastic idea. Juniper, on the other hand, thought it was foolish. She told me there weren't enough people in town who had peanut allergies to support a bakery specifically for them." Ada folded her arms and shrugged. "I tried to point out that not only people allergic to peanuts would shop there. I mean, everyone can eat peanut-free stuff. Juniper shot that idea down, too, saying that the town couldn't support three bakeries, especially when two of them were owned by trained pastry chefs. It's like she thought I wasn't a real pastry chef because I teach at a high school instead of at Le Cordon Bleu or something. Not that it mattered, I guess. She was insistent that she wasn't going to invest in something she was sure would be a failure. I loved Juniper, but she could be so pigheaded sometimes." She gave them a small smile. "I like to think that I could have changed her mind."

Tassie offered her a smile in return. "I'm sure you could have."

As they said their goodbyes, Jack waited until they were outside to say anything.

"Does that show of support back there about her changing Juniper's mind mean you don't think Ada did it?" he asked.

"I wouldn't say that." She stowed Baxter safely in his carrier in the backseat before looking at Jack. "Her friendship with Juniper seems sincere though, despite Juniper looking down on Ada's baking skills."

He winced. "Yeah, that was rough. Friends or not, that could give Ada motive."

"Especially if Ada thought she could use the inheritance Juniper left her to start that bakery she'd always dreamed of."

Chapter 13

"I was going to stop by and talk to Juniper's husband," Jack said as he pulled out of the school parking lot. "Do you and Baxter want to come with me?"

"Definitely," Tassie said. "I'm interested to see what he has to say about her."

Tassie expected Jack to head to the cliffs and the Larabee's majestic Victorian, but instead, a few minutes later, he parked in front of an accountant's office in town.

"Is this where Calvin works?" she asked.

Jack nodded. "He's a CPA here. When I called, I thought he'd want to meet me at their home, but he asked me to come to his office instead."

"Don't you think it's a little odd that everyone close to Juniper is going about their everyday lives like things are business as usual?" Tassie asked as she lifted Baxter out of his carrier. "Ada and Calvin are both working. Victoria is making videos. Her daughter, Elena, is the only one who seems to be taking some time to process what happened to Juniper."

"I'll admit, it *is* a little weird," Jack agreed.

And more than a little suspicious.

A red-haired receptionist was seated at the desk directly opposite the door and she looked up with a smile as they walked into the lobby. "May I help you?"

"We're here to see Calvin Larabee," Jack said.

"Go right back," the woman said. "First door on your right."

Calvin was on the phone when they got to his office and he muttered something into his cell about seeing whoever he was talking to later, then hung up and got to his feet. Gray-haired, he wore round wire-rimmed glasses that did little to hide his bloodshot eyes.

"Detective," he said, offering his hand.

"Thanks for seeing us." Jack shook his hand. "This is Tassie Drake. She's helping out with the investigation."

Tassie smiled. "Nice meeting you."

She expected Calvin to ask how she was assisting the police—or at the very least, how Baxter helped out—but instead, he merely nodded, clearly preoccupied. His meticulous desk seemed like a sharp contrast to his haggard appearance. Not a pen, paper, or folder looked out of place. The walls were bare and there wasn't a filing cabinet in sight, but perhaps all the accountants kept their paperwork in one central room. And as far as personal items went, he had a simple white coffee mug with the logo of the CPA firm on it and a photo of Juniper and Elena on his desk.

To Tassie, the whole office was rather stark and austere. Then again, she tended to like lots of knickknacks and other stuff around.

"Have a seat." Calvin gestured to the chairs in front of his desk. "When we talked on the phone, you said this was about Juniper. Have you found the killer yet?"

"Not yet, I'm afraid." Jack pulled out his notebook and took the chair beside Tassie. "We were hoping you might be able to help us with that."

Calvin's brow furrowed. "I'm not sure I'll be much help. I wasn't at the *Cupcake Combat* taping."

"That's okay," Jack said. "We're more interested in things that happened in the days before *Cupcake Combat*."

"Such as?"

"Did Juniper get into a fight with anyone?" Tassie asked.

"Anyone who knew Juniper knew she had a quick temper, so I'm sure she had an argument with someone." Calvin let out a heavy sigh. "I often wondered how Victoria could work with her."

Baxter's ears perked up at that. So did Tassie's.

"They didn't get along?" she asked.

"I wouldn't say that. They both had strong opinions about how things should be done, so they butted heads sometimes."

Jack frowned at that. "I'm a little confused. I thought Victoria was her assistant. Didn't she work for Juniper?"

Calvin leaned back in his chair. "Yes, but their relationship was complicated, to say the least. Juniper was the face of her business, but she wasn't very good at all the other stuff, which was why she hired an assistant. Victoria did everything for her, including writing the scripts for the videos, baking whatever they needed for the videos, answering emails and messages from fans, and taking care of Juniper's social media. They both had strong opinions about what Juniper should and shouldn't do. Victoria thought Juniper hurt her brand by some of the things she did."

"Like what, specifically?" Jack asked.

"Like the video Juniper made about *Cupcake Combat* and the bakers competing in it."

"The one where Juniper said all those mean things about Hazel," Tassie said.

Calvin's mouth tightened. "Yes. Victoria didn't write the script for that video, by the way. That was all Juniper."

Jack exchanged looks with Tassie before turning back to Calvin. "You sound like you didn't like the video."

"I didn't."

"Was it because she went after Hazel?" Tassie asked.

Calvin sat up, pinning her with a frown. "Why would you ask that?"

"Hazel told me that you and she were high school sweethearts," Tassie explained. "I just assumed you were still friends."

She really didn't assume that, but it seemed the most likely way to get him talking about his relationship with Hazel.

His mouth worked as he considered that. "Hazel and I had a rough breakup. When I went to college after graduation, she stayed in Bluewater Bay, and we drifted apart."

"But it must have worked out okay because then you started dating Juniper," Tassie said.

"It did." Calvin offered them a small smile. "I feel badly about hurting Hazel the way I did, but I can't apologize for falling in love with Juniper."

Tassie supposed she could understand that. After talking to Hazel, she still couldn't help feeling sorry for the woman, though. Calvin claimed he simply fell in love with Juniper, but from Hazel's perspective, Juniper stole Calvin from her. What really happened was probably somewhere in between and none of them would ever truly know. Perception was reality and all that.

"It sounds like your relationship was pretty solid," Jack remarked. "Why would Juniper still resent Hazel?"

"Despite the face she showed the online world, Juniper could be insecure," Calvin said. "When it came to Hazel and me, she always saw things that weren't there. Plain and simple, Juniper was jealous." He glanced at his watch. "Is there anything else, Detective? I promised my daughter I'd be home early. She's having a hard time with her mother's death."

Jack closed his notebook and put it away. "I think we're good right now. Thanks for your time."

"Of course." Calvin pushed back his chair and stood, coming around the desk to walk them to the door. "You'll keep me updated on the investigation?"

Jack nodded, assuring the man that he would.

"So, did our little lie detector alert on anything in there?" Jack asked when they got to his SUV.

Tassie had let Jack in on Baxter's amazing skill on their first murder investigation together. He'd thought she was pulling his leg—anyone would, right?—but then she'd played two truths and a lie with him and Baxter had given her his signature side-eye, tipping her off to which one was the lie. And yeah, it had pretty much blown Jack's mind.

"Not a thing," Tassie said even as Baxter smiled up at them. "That doesn't mean he didn't kill Juniper though. With all that money coming his way, he definitely had motive. And he had access to her purse."

"I agree." Jack took out his phone and glanced at the time. "I have to give my daily update to the mayor about the investigation."

"He makes you give him daily updates?"

Jack grimaced. "Yeah. It was the only way I could keep him from having a complete meltdown."

She didn't envy him that job. Fillmore was a doofus. "He's going to blame you if the *Cupcake Combat* people leave, isn't he?"

"Probably. But enough about Fillmore," Jack said with a grin. "I'd rather talk about the rain check for that date I owe you. What do you think about going out to dinner Friday night?"

Tassie opened her mouth to say she thought that sounded fun only to remember that she had to be somewhere else that night. She groaned.

"I'd love to, but Baxter and I are going to my parents' house for dinner for my brother's birthday," she said. At the confused look on Jack's face, she added, "They won't talk about him, and yet, they insist we get together and celebrate. My mom makes Nolan's favorite meal and dessert and everything. It's weird and painful, but my sister and I always go anyway."

Tassie considered asking Jack if he wanted to come to dinner with her but stopped herself. She and Jack hadn't even gone an official date yet. Turning dinner at her parents' into their first date would probably be all kinds of awkward.

She smiled. "Another rain check?"

"Yeah, of course." He flashed her another grin that made her pulse do a little dance. "Anytime."

Hopefully, that rain check didn't have a *Use By Date* on it. Because with their track record, something would probably come up.

Chapter 14

Tassie decided to walk back to Pupcakes from Calvin's accounting office, Baxter happily prancing along beside her. Not only was the sunny spring weather perfect for a stroll through town, but since he didn't have to drop them off, Jack wouldn't be late for his meeting with the mayor. Ugh. Fillmore was a blustering fool. She still wasn't sure how the man had gotten the job.

Poor Jack.

She couldn't help smiling as she thought about him. When he'd first gotten to Bluewater Bay, Lucy had wanted to play matchmaker and introduce them, but Tassie had talked her out of it. Her friend's track record hadn't been all that great when she'd tried to set Tassie up before. But after meeting Jack at the scene of a murder, Tassie was definitely interested. And while she was all for taking things slow with a guy, she was more than ready to go on a date with Jack.

Tassie was still thinking about the handsome detective when she realized she and Baxter were walking right past Irene's bakery, Dreamy Desserts. Maybe they should stop and talk to her and see if they could get to the bottom of what was going on between her and Gwen.

Before one of them framed the other for murder.

Baxter was all for that idea. Although, she suspected that might be because he loved how delicious Dreamy Desserts smelled. She certainly couldn't blame him. The aroma of cookies, cakes, pies, and donuts filled the bakery, making her hungry and reminding her that she hadn't eaten since lunch. That probably wouldn't be such a big deal if she weren't the kind of person who liked to nibble throughout the day. And the sight of all those yummy goodies in the display cases were tempting.

"Hey, Tassie! Hey, Baxter!"

Baxter wagged his tail in greeting as she smiled at the teenage girl who worked part-time at the bakery after school. "Hey, Ellie. Is Irene here?"

"She just stepped out to do some errands."

"Drats," Tassie muttered. "Can you tell her that I stopped by?"

The redhead nodded, her ponytail bobbing. "Sure thing!"

"Come on, Baxter," Tassie said. "Let's head back to Pupcakes."

It only took a few minutes to get to the shop, and when they walked in, Tassie was surprised to see Irene there. She'd picked out treats for her Shar Pei, Luna, and was just finishing up at the counter with Abby.

"Just the person I was looking for," Tassie said when Irene turned around. "I stopped by Dreamy Desserts a few minutes ago, but Ellie said you were out doing errands."

"Luna needed some treats." Irene smiled, reaching down to pet Baxter as he walked over to greet her. "What's up?"

That was when Tassie realized that she hadn't quite figured out how to best bring up the subject of Gwen to Irene. Oh, well. She'd have to make it up as she went. It wouldn't be the first time.

"I was talking to Gwen this morning..." she began.

Irene rolled her eyes. "What did she accuse me of now?"

Murder, for one thing.

Best not to mention that, Tassie thought. She didn't want to add any more fuel to the already raging dumpster fire.

"I hate seeing you and Gwen at odds with each other, so I wanted to know what happened between the two of you in high school," she said, then added, "When you used to be friends."

Irene chewed on her lower lip thoughtfully. "What did she say?"

"She said I should ask you."

Her friend let out a snort. "Typical."

Tassie stifled a groan. She'd hoped she wouldn't have to drag Irene kicking and screaming into this conversation, but obviously, Irene was going to be just as difficult as Gwen.

"So," she said. "Are you going to tell me?"

"It's a long story," Irene muttered.

Tassie made a show of looking around. There weren't any customers in the shop at the moment, and if someone did come in, she knew Abby would take care of them. "Well, I'm not doing anything right now."

When Irene folded her arms with a sigh, Tassie half expected her not to answer, but Irene surprised her. "Gwen blames me for not getting to go to Paris."

Tassie exchanged looks with Baxter. "Wait a minute. Back up. When was she supposed to go to Paris? And why does she blame you for not being able to go there?"

Irene sighed. "Gwen and I both wanted to be part of an exchange program to this fancy culinary school in Paris for pastry arts. You had to apply online, then after you were accepted—which we both were—you had to send in your registration by snail mail to their small satellite school in New York City."

"Wow. That's cool."

Tassie couldn't remember Ada mentioning the exchange program in the culinary class she'd taken. Maybe Ada didn't think she'd been a good fit. She wouldn't have been wrong. Tassie could bake—her specialty being doggy treats—but no one would mistake her for a world-renowned pastry chef.

"It was," Irene agreed, then grimaced. "Or it would have been. I got my confirmation letter from the satellite school right away, but Gwen didn't, and when she called the school to check, they said they never received her registration. Gwen was frantic and upset. We both were.

She was my best friend and I wanted her to go to Paris with me as much as she did."

"What happened?"

Irene shrugged. "I still don't know. We both put our registrations in the mailbox in front of her house, but when we checked with their usual mail carrier, he said there was only one envelope in there—mine. Which didn't make sense because her boyfriend and I were there when Gwen and I put both envelopes in the box."

"That's weird."

"Right?" Irene shook her head. "Anyway, Gwen accused me of going back out to the mailbox later and stealing the envelope with her registration."

Tassie supposed she should have seen that coming, especially since Irene already said that Gwen blamed her for not being able to go to Paris, but still. That was a little out there.

"Seriously?"

Irene nodded. "She claimed I didn't want her to go because I was afraid she would turn out to be the better baker. I told her I would never do something like that but she didn't believe me."

"Why didn't Gwen just send in her registration again?"

"Because she missed the deadline. We haven't been friends since." Irene sighed. "I didn't take her registration, Tassie. I don't know what happened to it, but I promise you, I didn't take it."

"I know you didn't," Tassie said.

She glanced at Baxter for confirmation, then immediately felt badly about thinking Irene was lying in the first place. But hey, she was trying to patch up a friendship here. She needed to be sure.

"Maybe Gwen's boyfriend from high school might be able to help figure out what happened," she said. "Who was she dating?"

"Wyatt Hicks."

"Oh, that's right!" Tassie was pretty sure he'd played football. Or maybe basketball. "Do you know if he still lives in Bluewater Bay?"

"Yup. He works at his family's grocery store."

"I think I'll talk to him," Tassie said. "See if he remembers anything."

Irene nodded, offering her a small smile. "I appreciate what you're trying to do, but unless you have something that proves I didn't sabotage Gwen's dream of going to Paris, I don't think she's going to believe you."

"Then I'll find proof."

"I hope so. Then maybe Gwen will stop telling everyone in town that I murdered Juniper."

Tassie blinked. "Is that what she's doing?"

Irene nodded. "I don't think most people believe her, but what if Detective Sterling does?"

"He won't," Tassie assured her. At least, she didn't think he would. "You didn't have a fight with Juniper before she was killed, did you?"

Irene hesitated. "Define what you mean by a fight."

Tassie let out a groan. "You did, didn't you?"

"I didn't mean to," Irene protested. "I asked her to have coffee with me at Hug in a Mug. I wanted to butter her up so that she'd pick me to win *Cupcake Combat* Champion over Gwen—because we all know that she wasn't going to allow Hazel to win—but she got all offended, and I ended up saying some things to her that I shouldn't have said. Unfortunately, everyone at Hug in a Mug heard me say them, too."

"Oh, Irene."

"I know, I know. But I couldn't let Gwen win. If she did, she'd do nothing but crow about it. In fact," Irene added, "I wouldn't be surprised if Gwen murdered Juniper."

Tassie should have known Irene would go there sooner or later.

"Why do you think Gwen killed her?"

"Because Gwen wants to win *Cupcake Combat* as much as I do, and she'd do anything to be crowned champion."

Tassie was pretty sure that *anything* didn't include murder, but Irene wasn't ready to see it that way.

Yet.

"I have to get back to the bakery," Irene said. "Let me know if Gwen's old boyfriend is able to shed any light on what happened to her registration."

"I will." Tassie smiled. "Tell Luna that we said hi."

Irene promised she would as she went out the door.

"Go ahead and go," Abby said.

Tassie turned to look at her sister. "What?"

"Go talk to Wyatt. I've got things covered here."

"Are you sure? I was out a lot today."

She really wanted to talk to Gwen's old boyfriend, but at the same time, she did have a shop to take care of.

"And I'll be out all day with Isaac tomorrow," Abby reminded her. "Besides, we need more cinnamon chai tea."

Her sister had a point. "Have you decided what you guys are doing for your date yet?"

She should probably start coming up with a list of ideas in case she and Jack actually ever went out.

"We're taking the pups hiking, then to the beach," her sister said.

"Sounds fun."

Baxter must have thought so, too, because he grinned up at them. Tassie reached down to caress his ears. She wasn't much of the outdoor type, so hiking was probably out. Though she did love going to the beach. Maybe she'd suggest to Jack that they take Baxter and Gus sometime.

"So, go talk to Wyatt." Abby smiled. "I'd like to see Gwen and Irene get back to being friends, too, so go."

Tassie grinned. "You're the best."

"I know."

Chapter 15

Hicks Grocery was Bluewater Bay's go-to for food shopping. Bright and airy, it might not be as big as the chain grocery stores, but it had everything you could get at those places, including an outstanding produce section, which just so happened to be the department where Wyatt worked.

Once inside, Tassie guided Baxter toward the fruits and veggies part of the store. His nose worked overtime as he sniffed the apples, oranges, bananas, and all the other fresh produce as they walked past the displays, tail wagging happily.

Tassie was so focused on looking for Wyatt that she almost didn't see Lucy over by the green grapes. Baxter, on the other hand, spotted her right away.

"Hey!" Tassie said, walking over to her friend.

Lucy gave her a smile as she placed a big bag of grapes in her shopping cart. "Hey, yourself. Hey, Baxter."

He wagged his tail faster in greeting.

"How's my goddaughter doing today?" Tassie asked with a grin.

Lucy caressed her belly with her hand, her expression softening. "Excited to meet everyone. Especially Bruno. Whenever she's restless, Bruno comes over to sit beside me, and Flower immediately chills out."

"Awww. That's so sweet."

And not at all surprising. Pets were amazing at sensing what their humans needed.

"Where's your cart?" Lucy asked, looking around.

"Oh, we're not here shopping. Well, other than to get some cinnamon chai tea. We're mostly here to talk to Wyatt, Gwen's old boyfriend from high school." She told Lucy what Irene said, adding, "Hopefully, he'll be able to help figure out what happened."

"That'd be nice. This thing with Gwen and Irene is getting old." Lucy leaned her hip against the produce case. "Speaking of things that'd be nice, when are you and Jack finally going out on an actual date?"

At the question, Baxter looked at Tassie quizzically.

"Well, we were going to have dinner after the *Cupcake Combat* taping the other day, but you know how that turned out," Tassie said. "Then Jack asked if I wanted to get together tomorrow night, but Baxter and I are going to Mom and Dad's for Nolan's birthday."

"Ah." Lucy knew all about her brother mysteriously leaving home and how her parents celebrated his birthday even after he'd left. "Did you ask Jack to go with you?"

Tassie made a face. "I wanted to, but I figured that might be kind of weird so I asked him for a rain check."

"You should have asked him if he's free another night instead."

"I don't think that's how rain checks work," Tassie said. "I think the person who gets rain checked is supposed to suggest the next date."

The minute she said it, she realized that Jack was the one who'd asked for a rain check for their first date and had also suggested their second date. So, maybe that rule didn't apply? It seemed like it should, though.

"I'm pretty sure there aren't any hard and fast rules when it comes to rain checks," Lucy drawled.

"Sure there are."

Lucy took out her phone. "I'm going to check."

"What are you going to do, Google it?"

"Yup."

Tassie couldn't help being amused as Lucy proceeded to do exactly that. Admittedly, she Googled a lot of stuff too, but hadn't ever thought of looking up rain check etiquette. It was actually a good idea.

"Hmm." Lucy scrunched up her face as she read. "This person believes if you ask for the rain check, then it's up to you to suggest another date. Another person says you should suggest another date, but you don't necessarily have to. There's also someone who insists that if you rain check a guy, you should give him dates and times that you're available for another date, but if you didn't—and he's into you—he'll almost certainly ask you out again, so don't worry about it."

"Well, that was a waste of time," Tassie grumbled. "Those answers are all over the place."

"Which means I was right and that there aren't any rules when it comes to rain checking someone." Lucy slipped her phone back into her big, oversized purse. "The bottom line is you showed Jack that you're still interested by asking for a rain check and he's still interested by accepting the rain check. I think you're good."

That was a relief. Because asking him as an afterthought to her parents' house for dinner now would be even weirder.

Lucy jabbed a finger in her direction. "But if you rain check him again, suggest another date, okay?"

Tassie laughed. "I will. Promise. Let's just hope I don't need to rain check him again."

Because while there might not be rules when it came to rain checks, there might very well be a limit to how many of those aforementioned rain checks you could use.

Baxter booped Tassie's leg with his nose, getting her attention. She glanced down to see him focused on the other side of the produce section where Wyatt was adding a fresh shipment of vine-ripened red tomatoes to the display. Tall and thin with dark blond hair, he wore a dark green apron with Hicks Grocery embroidered on it over a pair of khakis and a polo shirt.

Ah, yes. She remembered now. Yup, he'd definitely played basketball in high school.

"Good job, Baxter." She reached down to pet his cute little head, then looked at Lucy. "There's Wyatt. I'll talk to you later. Tell Andrew and Bruno that Baxter and I said hi."

"I will," Lucy said.

Wyatt looked up when she and Baxter walked over. "Can I help you find something today?"

"I'm actually looking for you." She smiled. "Tassie Drake. We went to high school together."

He eyed her for a moment, like he was trying to place her. "Oh, yeah. That's right. You were the girl who passed out in bio when we dissected frogs."

Tassie cringed. "That's me."

Yeah, that was probably her most embarrassing moment. It was also why she couldn't follow in her parents' footsteps and go to veterinary school. She was pretty squeamish when it came to stuff like that. Even now, the thought of that poor frog pinned to that dissection tray made her knees all rubbery.

"So, why were you looking for me?" Wyatt asked.

"I wanted to talk to you about Gwen."

He frowned. "What about Gwen?"

"You went out with her in high school, right?"

Something that looked like pain flickered in Wyatt's eyes, but he went back to stacking tomatoes before she could be sure, carefully placing each of them on the pile. "Yeah."

"Do you remember when Gwen was going to go to that pastry school in Paris?"

"What about it?"

Tassie related what Irene had told her. When she was finished, Wyatt stopped stacking tomatoes and looked at her.

"Why are we talking about something that happened in high school?" he asked.

"I'm just trying to figure out what happened to that envelope. Gwen thinks Irene took it, and I'm just trying to figure out if she did." Tassie smiled. "I can't help myself. I love a good mystery."

He didn't say anything as he went back to what he'd been doing.

"Were you there when Gwen and Irene put the envelopes in the mailbox?" she asked.

"Yeah, I was there."

"Do you think Irene took Gwen's registration?" Tassie asked.

He shrugged. "I don't know what happened to it."

Beside Tassie, Baxter gave her the side-eye, letting her know that Wyatt was lying.

That was interesting.

Who was he protecting?

It couldn't be Irene because Gwen was already convinced she did it, so what would be the harm in confirming it?

Tassie thought a moment, trying to figure out how to get him to admit what he knew.

"I know it's been a while but are you sure?" she finally asked. "If you saw Irene take the envelope, you can tell me."

"I didn't see Irene take it," he said firmly.

Tassie pretended to think about that. "It doesn't mean she didn't take it. She could have come back to the mailbox any time before the mail carrier picked it up. It wouldn't have been all that difficult. It would have been super easy to pretend she was checking the mail while what she was actually doing was stealing Gwen's envelope."

For a long time, Wyatt stared down at the box of tomatoes on the cart that he hadn't unpacked yet before finally looking at her.

"Irene didn't take Gwen's envelope," he said quietly.

"How can you be sure?"

"Because I took it."

Okay. Tassie hadn't expected that.

Sitting beside her, Baxter looked as stunned as she was.

"Why would you take it?" she asked incredulously.

Wyatt sighed. "Because I didn't want Gwen to go to Paris. I thought that if she did, she'd end up meeting some suave French guy and dump me." He let out a snort. "It didn't matter, though, because she broke up with me a few days after Irene left anyway."

Tassie gaped at him, trying to wrap her mind around that.

"I'm not proud of what I did, okay? I feel terrible about it to this day," he said in frustration. "But once I did it, I couldn't undo it."

"So you let Gwen think Irene took it."

Wyatt winced. "I never thought she'd think that. They were friends."

Tassie wouldn't have thought Gwen would jump to that conclusion either, but the minute she did, Wyatt should have come clean with her.

"You need to tell Gwen the truth," she said firmly.

He looked horrified at the thought. "I can't do that! She'll hate me."

Tassie pinned him with a look. "Better Gwen hate you than hate Irene when she didn't do anything wrong."

Wyatt reeled back like she'd smacked him.

"I'm sorry. That was harsh," Tassie said with a sigh. "But Gwen and Irene are both my friends, and I don't like seeing them hurt each other."

He drew himself up, took a deep breath, then nodded. "You're right. I need to tell Gwen the truth. Going to Paris for pastry arts was her dream and I took that from her."

"Yes, you did," Tassie agreed.

Wyatt gave her an embarrassed look. "Do you think you could talk to Gwen first? You know, to kind of soften her up a little for me?"

Tassie ran her tongue over her teeth as she considered that. She'd already inserted herself into the situation, so was this that much of an ask?

"Okay," she finally said. "I'll talk to Gwen first, but then you'd better be prepared to apologize to her yourself."

"Do you think Gwen will ever forgive me?"

Considering she still hadn't forgiven Irene when Gwen thought she'd sabotaged her, Tassie was thinking that was probably going to be a hard no. But she didn't say that. For all she knew, she could be completely off the mark on that. Maybe Gwen would forgive him.

The real question was, would Irene forgive Gwen for accusing her of derailing her dream?

Chapter 16

After getting a promise from Wyatt that he'd talk to Gwen, Tassie and Baxter headed back to Pupcakes. As their walk took them past the park, she noted that the *Cupcake Combat* stuff wasn't there now. That wasn't surprising, she supposed. It wasn't like they could leave the kitchens out there. She hoped they still taped the show. While she felt awful about what had happened to Juniper, she also felt bad about Gwen, Irene, and Hazel not being able to compete. They were the reason *Cupcake Combat* had come to Bluewater Bay.

Tassie glanced over at the park again only to stop in her tracks when she spotted Calvin and Hazel sitting on one of the benches, their heads together.

Well, that wasn't suspicious at all.

Wanting to spy on them but not *look* like she was spying on them, Tassie quickly picked Baxter up and turned around, pretending to look in one of the store windows so she could watch them.

"It won't look weird if you watch them," she said to Baxter. "Let me know if you see something I don't."

Okay, maybe Calvin and Hazel sitting together in the park talking wasn't all that suspicious. If it was, would they be out in a public place where anyone could see? If Calvin murdered Juniper, would he really be so bold as to be seen in public with Hazel? Or maybe they were doing precisely that so people wouldn't think it was suspicious.

Drats.

It would be nice if she could hear what Calvin and Hazel were saying. Because, really, they could be discussing anything.

"What do you think they're talking about?" she asked Baxter. "Maybe Calvin is apologizing for the nasty stuff Juniper said about Hazel on her video. Or maybe Hazel is suggesting they rekindle their high school romance. On the other hand, they could also be wondering what we're doing standing in front of a store that sells tourist stuff."

Yeah, it was probably that one.

Well, she wasn't going to learn anything incriminating one way or another by watching them.

"Okay, come on, baby."

Sighing, Tassie turned, Baxter still in her arms, when she saw Calvin slowly and casually—and quite frankly, furtively—reach over and take Hazel's hand, giving it a squeeze.

"Did you see that?" Tassie asked Baxter.

He booped her nose in answer.

"Now, *that* was definitely suspicious," she said.

Were Calvin and Hazel getting back together? Had one of them murdered Juniper? Had both of them? Or had neither of them killed her and were they simply taking advantage of her death?

That last possibility was kind of cringy.

Giving them one more look, Tassie set Baxter on the sidewalk and started toward Pupcakes. Abby was just cleaning up the kitchen when they got there and Tassie filled her in on what she'd learned from Wyatt. To say her sister was surprised was putting it mildly.

"Are you going to tell Gwen?" Abby asked.

"Yeah. I'm just not sure if it's going to fix anything between them."

Since Abby was having dinner with Isaac, Tassie told her that she'd mind the shop for the rest of the day, then close up. On the way home, she stopped by The General Store to pick up a grilled chicken salad with avocado and dressing on the side for dinner, then ate in front of the TV with Baxter on the couch beside her, the two of them watching *Murder She Wrote*. Not only was it one of her favorite all-time shows, but Tassie hoped the show's sleuth, Jessica Fletcher, might give her some insight into solving Juniper's murder. Unfortunately, while she enjoyed the episode—which she'd already seen about twenty times—she didn't get any inspiration from Jessica.

"I'm going to call Jack and tell him about what we saw in the park," Tassie said after she'd finished eating and had put her plate in the dishwasher.

Baxter must have liked that idea because he settled himself beside her again and got comfortable when she curled up on the couch with her phone.

"You know what? I'm going to FaceTime him instead. That way I can see his expression when I tell him about Calvin and Hazel."

And she'd get to look at that handsome face.

Finding Jack in her list of favorites, she tapped the FaceTime icon. He answered right away.

"Hey," he said, flashing her a grin.

"Hey. I'm not bothering you, am I?"

"You could never bother me. Besides, I'm just making dinner. What's up?"

Tassie wasn't sure why, but she assumed Jack would still be at the police station. Eager to get a glimpse of his place, she took in the white cabinets and fridge behind him. When she turned her attention back to him, he was dumping a whole box of pasta in a pot of boiling water.

"Are you having company?" she asked.

She was curious partly because she didn't want to keep him if he had guests, but mostly because she wanted to know if that guest was of the feminine persuasion.

Jack looked confused for a second. "No. Why would you think I'm having company?"

"Because you're cooking a whole box of pasta."

He stared at the box still in his free hand, looking even more perplexed now. "Yeah..."

"You know that's not a single serving box, right?"

He regarded the box for a moment, then shrugged. "If it was a single serving box, there'd be some way to reseal it."

Tassie laughed. That was guy logic if she'd ever heard it. She considered pointing out that they made plastic—or even glass—containers for all that pasta you didn't cook right away, but didn't. He'd probably just say it'd take up too much space in the cabinets or something.

Well, at least he wasn't sharing all that pasta with a date.

"How was your conversation with the mayor?" she asked.

Jack let out a snort. "The usual. He wants Juniper's murderer in jail yesterday."

"I figured. Baxter and I might have something to help narrow down our suspects."

He turned to lean back against the counter, giving her a look at what was almost certainly the living room if the huge TV over the fireplace was any indication. "What do you have?"

She caressed Baxter's head, smiling at him when he glanced up at her before turning his attention back to the phone where Jack was waiting patiently.

"Well, Baxter and I were walking past the park this afternoon when we saw Calvin and Hazel together," she explained. "They were sitting on a bench talking."

"Did you hear what they were saying?"

"No. Baxter and I were across the street. But we did see them covertly hold hands."

Jack crossed his free arm under the one with the phone, brow furrowing as he considered what she'd told him. "That's a little suspicious."

Tassie bobbed her head. "That's what I said!"

"Too bad you couldn't have eavesdropped on them."

"I know." She made a face. "But I was more concerned about Calvin and Hazel seeing us. I had to spy on them using a store window so I could see their reflection."

"That was smart."

"It was Baxter's idea." She grinned. "You know what this means."

"What?"

"That Calvin lied to us when he said he told Elena he'd be home early."

Jack frowned. "Baxter didn't alert on it when Calvin said it."

Drats.

That was true. He didn't.

"Then maybe Calvin did tell Elena he'd be home early when he really intended to meet up with Hazel instead," she suggested. "He wasn't technically lying so that's why Baxter didn't give us the look."

"I'll buy that," Jack said. "But Calvin could simply have also run into Hazel in the park and they stopped to talk."

It was Tassie's turn to frown. "Is this your way of telling me that you don't think either of them murdered Juniper?"

"No. This is my way of telling you that's what Calvin and Hazel will say if I ask them about it."

"Oh. I suppose that makes sense," she said. "But now that Juniper is no longer in the picture, it seems like Calvin and Hazel are picking up where they left off in high school. Which means that one of them could be the killer."

"Or both of them," Jack said. "Speaking of suspects, I'm going to talk to Gwen and Irene tomorrow. I thought you might want to tag along."

"I can't. Abby is taking off to spend the day with Isaac, so I have to mind the store." She chewed on her lip. "Neither of them killed Juniper, you know."

He shrugged. "Maybe not, but I still have to talk to them."

Tassie let out a sigh. "I know. Gwen and Irene already told me they think the other did it, so just keep their feud in mind when you talk to them, okay?"

His mouth edged up. "I will."

Although, at this rate, she was ready to lock both Gwen and Irene in a jail cell and tell them they couldn't come out until they settled their differences.

Hmm.

Wonder if Jack would go for that?

Chapter 17

Tassie was surprised when Jack walked into Pup-cakes a little before noon the next day. He hadn't said anything about stopping by before they'd hung up after talking last night. She was glad he had though. She liked hanging out with him.

She smiled. "Hey!"

Jack stopped to pet Baxter, who'd immediately hurried over to greet him with tail wagging, before walking over to the counter.

"Is that what I think it is?" she asked, gesturing to the pizza box in his hand with the very recognizable logo of The General Store on top.

He grinned. "If you think it's lunch, then yes. You haven't eaten yet, have you?"

"Nope. I've been busy all morning with customers and I'm starving. Let me put the *Closed for Lunch* sign on the door, then we can go into the break room."

She and Abby only closed for lunch when one of them was minding the store by themselves. Otherwise, they took turns eating. But pizza with Jack definitely called for some privacy.

Tassie came around the counter and was halfway to the door when a thought occurred to her. Stopping, she turned to look at him.

"You're staying for lunch, right?"

"I'd planned on it, yeah."

Tassie was hoping he'd say that. She gave him a smile. "Good."

"I asked Lucy what I should get you and she said you love their barbecue chicken pizza," Jack said as he followed her and Baxter into the break room, her pup glancing up at the delicious smelling box in his hand every few steps.

She did. "That's perfect."

If Jack talked to Lucy that meant having lunch with her wasn't a spur-of-the-moment thing. Did that mean this was a date? Now, she wished she'd worn something a little fancier than jeans and a tee with the name of her shop on it. But, in her defense, it *was* casual Friday.

The break room was part kitchenette and part doggy playroom and she had to slalom her way through the stuffed doggy toys on the floor. The big plush chairs, comfy dog donut beds, and colorful decor were eclectic to say the least, but it all worked.

"I see you have your murder board all set up," Jack said as he set the pizza box on the low table in front of a pair of lavender-colored stuffed chairs.

She glanced at the whiteboard on the far wall. "Yeah. As you can see, I haven't done much with it yet other than put names and pictures up there. Baxter and I are going to work on it in between customers this afternoon."

"The pictures are a nice touch."

Tassie turned away from the small sink where she'd just finished washing her hands to see Jack sitting down in one of the two chairs.

"Hey, don't make fun of my murder board," she said, taking two bottles of water out of the small fridge and handing him one as she slid into the other chair.

A teasing smile tugged playfully at his mouth. "I didn't make fun of it."

Sitting on the floor beside her, Baxter gave her the side-eye.

She gave Jack a smug look as she opened the pizza box. "Baxter doesn't believe you and neither do I. And as for the pictures of the suspects on the murder board, amateur detectives on TV always put them up."

Helping herself to a slice of pizza, she took a bite, then slowly chewed, daring him to say anything more about it. Instead, he chuckled and reached for his own slice.

"Speaking of suspects, I talked to Gwen and Irene this morning," he said. "Separately, of course."

"What did you think?"

"That there are better suspects to focus on."

She let out a sigh. "That's a relief."

He took a drink of water. "You were right about Gwen pointing her finger at Irene and vice versa. They really don't like each other."

"On the bright side, I now know why they don't," Tassie said, telling him what Irene had told her followed by her conversation with Wyatt.

"So, this whole thing is because Gwen's high school boyfriend didn't want her to go to Paris?" Jack asked incredulously.

"Yup. And now he wants me to be the one to tell Gwen so she won't hate him."

Jack snorted. "Are you going to?"

She nibbled on the crust, considering that. "Normally, I wouldn't, but I want Gwen and Irene to bury the hatchet—preferably not in each other—so yeah. I'm just not sure how to get Gwen and Irene in the same room together long enough to make this work."

"Ask each of them to meet you separately but give both of them the same time so that they have no choice but to talk to each other," he suggested.

She blinked at him. "So, I should ambush them, you mean."

Jack helped himself to another slice of pizza with a shrug. "Pretty much."

Tassie weighed the pros and cons of that suggestion. Gwen and Irene would both feel blindsided and be angry, but what other choice did she have? And if it got them to stop bickering, the subterfuge would be worth it.

She grinned. "You know, that just might work. Thanks for the idea."

Jack left to go back to the station about twenty minutes later, telling her and Baxter to have a good time at her parents that night. She thanked him, wishing once again she would have thought to ask him to come to dinner with them. But there was nothing to be done for it now.

"Okay, Baxter," she said. "Let's get to work on that murder board."

Going back into the break room, Tassie picked up the dry erase marker, then promptly stared at the names and pictures on the whiteboard. She didn't care if Jack made fun of her. The pictures she'd printed out of each suspect helped her think.

"Okay, Baxter," she said. "Let's go over what we know so far. Sound good?"

Her fur baby gazed up at her, that cute little white fur on his chin making it look like he was grinning.

Tassie grinned back at him before turning to the whiteboard. She focused on the picture of Juniper's assistant.

"On the surface, Victoria seemed to love Juniper. In fact, she had nothing but nice things to say about her employer. And she appeared to be genuinely shocked when Jack told her that Juniper was murdered. But she was also quick to take over Juniper's YouTube channel, almost like she'd already planned to do so."

As she spoke, Tassie wrote notes under the photo she'd printed out of Victoria. When she was done, she took a step back, reading what she'd jotted down.

"But is wanting to take over Juniper's channel enough of a motive? According to Calvin, her relationship with Juniper was complicated. Victoria did all the work for those videos and took care of Juniper's social media. She also didn't like a lot of the stuff Juniper did and thought she was ruining the brand. Maybe Victoria was tired of doing all the work and getting none of the credit, so she decided to kill Juniper. And she had access to Juniper's lip gloss and auto-injectors."

After making a note of all of that, Tassie moved to the next photo.

"Okay, what about Hazel?"

She glanced at Baxter to see him shift his focus from the picture of Victoria to the one of Hazel. So smart.

"Hazel had motive, that's for sure," Tassie said, turning her attention back to the whiteboard. "From her perspective, Juniper stole the man she loved. Now, Hazel said she was over it, but is she really? And what about that video Juniper made where she said some extremely unflattering things about Hazel? It wouldn't have been as easy for her to slip the tainted lip gloss and tampered auto-injectors in Juniper's bag as it was for Victoria, but she could still very well be at the top of the list of suspects. Plus, Melissa overheard her say that she wasn't going to let Juniper keep her from winning *Cupcake Combat*. Oh, and we did see her with Calvin in the park yesterday, looking pretty cozy."

Tassie tapped the picture of Juniper's husband. "Which brings us to Calvin. He seemed committed to Juniper, but clearly thought she went too far saying that stuff about Hazel on her video. Then we see him holding hands with Hazel in the park. While he obviously chose Juniper over Hazel in high school, maybe he changed his mind again. Maybe he wanted Juniper out of the way so he could get back together with Hazel. Switching out the lip gloss and auto-injectors would definitely have been simple."

She quickly finished writing all of that beneath Calvin's picture before looking at the one of Ada.

"Then there's Juniper's friend, Ada." Tassie glanced at Baxter. "Ada was one of my favorite teachers in high school, so it's weird to think she could be a murderer. She was super quick to point the finger at Hazel, though. And she did seem miffed about Juniper not opening that bakery with her. She also had access to Juniper's purse."

Tassie sighed. "And lastly, there's Juniper's daughter, Elena. I find it difficult to believe she murdered her mother. I know she resented Juniper for putting her online fame above everything else in her life—including her family—but Elena was genuinely distraught when we talked to her the other day. Of course, it's always possible that Elena was upset because she actually did kill Juniper and now regrets it, which is why I have her on the list."

With that, Tassie stepped back to survey the murder board, hoping something would jump out to her. It was still as muddled as before.

"Okay," she said. "Victoria, Calvin, Ada, and Elena all had easy access to Juniper's purse, and they all had motive. And while it would have been more difficult for Hazel to put something in Juniper's purse than anyone else, she also might have had the biggest motive. So, which one of them did it?"

She glanced at Baxter to see him gazing at the murder board intently.

"Yeah, I agree. It would be much easier to figure out who killed Juniper if an alibi would discount some of the suspects, but it won't because any one of them could have slipped the tainted lip gloss and empty auto-injectors into her purse at any time. I guess that means we'll have to do some more investigating."

But where did they start?

Chapter 18

Tassie supposed she could be a little biased, but she was of the opinion that her mom and dad were the best parents anyone could ever have, so she always loved going to their house for dinner. It didn't hurt that her mother was an amazing cook. But the vibe whenever they "celebrated" Nolan's birthday tended to be weird, to say the least. It made her wonder why they bothered. On some level, she could understand it. They all missed Nolan. But her parents took quiet and withdrawn to a whole new level on her brother's birthday. She didn't know if that was because they were busy thinking about why Nolan left, wondering where he was now and what he was doing, or whether they were bracing themselves for her and Abby to bring him up in conversation, and they'd all end up fighting.

But tonight, the vibe in their cozy Cape Cod–style house that was her beloved childhood home was different.

Tonight, her mom and dad were as talkative and fun as they normally were. Maybe it was because Abby had brought Isaac with her—which made Tassie once again wish she'd asked Jack to come to dinner—and they had to play the gracious hosts. If that was it, she'd have to remember to thank her sister for bringing her boyfriend because it meant she could enjoy the excellent Yankee pot roast her mom had made without being on pins and needles the whole time. The savory meal of chuck roast, baby carrots, potatoes, and pearl onions wasn't only Nolan's favorite. Tassie loved it too.

So did Baxter. Well, he and Finn, along with her parents' Weimaraner, Earl Gray, and Isaac's Pitbull mix, Rufus, couldn't eat any of it, of course, but they clearly enjoyed sitting near their humans' respective chairs appreciating the aroma.

"So, when are your father and I going to meet Jack?" her mother asked.

Tassie looked up from her plate in surprise, a forkful of pot roast halfway to her mouth, to see her mom regarding her expectantly from one end of the dining room table. On the opposite end, her father seemed just as curious. Considering that everyone else in town seemed to know about her and Jack, she supposed she shouldn't be stunned her parents knew as well. That said, she still hadn't expected the question.

Beside Tassie's chair, Baxter looked up at her like he was interested in the answer too.

"Well," she stammered. "We haven't actually gone on a date yet."

"Yes, you have," Abby said from where she sat across from Tassie. "Actually, you've gone on lots of dates with him."

Tassie frowned. "No, I haven't."

"What about all the times you and Jack go out investigating?" Abby asked.

"Those weren't dates!"

"Not traditional dates, maybe, but they're dates, all the same." Her sister gave her a superior look. "Besides, he brought you lunch today. That was definitely a date."

Tassie gaped. "How do you know he bought me lunch?"

"Lucy told me."

Tassie groaned silently. Of course she did. Lucy probably had a group text devoted exclusively to Tassie's love life.

Sitting beside Abby, her good-looking blond-haired boyfriend, Isaac, watched the back and forth between her and her sister in what seemed like genuine amusement. As for her mom and dad, they both looked baffled.

Her mother held up her hand. An older version of Tassie and Abby, she pinned Tassie with a look. "Wait a minute. What does Abby mean, investigating?"

"Tassie helped Jack solve Conrad Meyers' murder," Abby said.

"Helped him how?" her father asked, dark eyes curious behind his wire-rimmed glasses.

Shrugging in an effort to downplay the whole thing, Tassie speared a baby carrot with her fork. "I didn't really do all that much. Baxter and I merely talked to some of the people who we thought were suspects. All the evidence pointed to Sara and I wanted to help clear her name."

She didn't mention that she was the one who'd found Conrad's body and that's how she and Jack met. She was sure it would come out at some point. Maybe after she and Jack had been dating a while.

Yeah, she was thinking ahead.

"That isn't all you did," Abby protested. "You saved Jack's life."

"Saved his life?" Isaac said, looking at her in surprise. "What'd you do?"

Tassie groaned. She knew the incident Abby was talking about and would much prefer if her parents never found out about it. But she wasn't sure how she could be casual about those events, not with Abby sitting right there clearly ready to spill the proverbial beans.

"I didn't do anything that amazing. We were up at Waverly Lake checking out a cabin for evidence when the killer started shooting at us," she said, explaining what happened in as little detail as she could while at the same time giving Abby a pointed look. "Jack was the one who saved my life and Baxter's. I didn't do much more than duck my head and run."

"You're being modest," Abby said. "There was no way I could have done what you did. You were like a superhero!"

Tassie certainly didn't think of a superhero and would have told her sister as much if she wasn't so focused on the horrified expressions on her parents' faces.

This was exactly why she didn't want her mom and dad knowing about what happened. Tassie couldn't be mad at her sister, though. Well, she would be if she thought Abby had done it simply to be a nuisance. But Abby had told them because she was genuinely proud of her. How could Tassie be angry at her for that?

"We heard about what happened at Waverly Lake, but I had no idea you were there, Tassie," her mother said before looking at her father. "Did you know about this?"

He shook his head, mouth tight. "No, I didn't. Tassie, do you really think you should be involved in this kind of stuff? It's sounds more than a little dangerous."

"You sound like Jack," Tassie muttered.

"Then he must be a smart man," her father said.

"He is." Tassie gave her father a small smile she hoped was reassuring. "Dad, that was an unusual situation. Most of the time, all Baxter and I do is talk to people and bounce ideas around with Jack." Resisting the urge to glance at Baxter to see if he gave her the side-eye, she turned to her mother. "Really, Mom."

Neither of her parents looked very convinced, but thankfully, both seemed willing to let it go for the moment.

"Are you helping Jack with Juniper's murder, too?" her mom asked.

Tassie slathered a piece of pot roast in gravy, picking up a raisin with it. Raisins were her mother's secret ingredient in the dish and they added the perfect amount of sweetness. "Yeah, but we aren't making much progress yet."

"Why not?" her dad asked.

"Because any of the suspects could have killed her." She sighed. "You guys didn't know Juniper, did you?"

"No." Her mom picked up her glass of water and took a sip. "But one of our vet techs is friends with Juniper's assistant—I think her name is Victoria?"

Her parents had their own veterinary practice in Bluewater Bay, appropriately named The Doctors Drake. She had them to thank for her love of dogs. Just another thing that made them awesome.

Tassie nodded. "Yes, that's her name. Did she mention whether Victoria ever said anything to her about Juniper."

"Now, this is second-hand information, but according to her, Victoria thought Juniper had lied to her. Victoria worked all hours of the day and night with the understanding that Juniper would help her launch her own career, but Juniper never made good on that promise."

Huh.

"That's interesting. Especially since Victoria has pretty much already taken over Juniper's channel and is starting to make it her own," Tassie said. "I'll mention it to Jack."

And add it to the murder board back at Pupcakes.

They talked a little more about Juniper's murder as they finished dinner—and a lot more about Jack— before Tassie volunteered to clear the table with Abby and get dessert, Baxter prancing at her side.

Like the rest of the house, the modern kitchen was light and airy with an island separating it from the dining room and living room. While their parents and Isaac could see her and Abby from where they were sitting, they couldn't hear what she and her sister were talking about if they kept their voices soft enough.

Which they needed to do with the conversation she and Abby were going to have.

"I don't think we should mention Nolan to Mom and Dad tonight," Tassie said, her voice near a whisper as she took the homemade sweetened whipped cream out of the fridge to pair with the fresh blueberry cobbler their mother had made.

Abby looked at her in surprise. "You don't?"

Tassie glanced over at the table where their parents and Isaac were laughing about something before she turned back to her sister. "We're having such a good time that I don't want to mess with that by bringing him up. I think it's better to talk to them about Nolan another time."

"I agree."

The relief in her sister's voice was obvious. Tassie had to admit, she was relieved, too. She hadn't been looking forward to that discussion. And with her newfound sleuthing skills, it might be better—and easier—for her to figure out why Nolan left another way instead of asking their parents.

Bowls, spoons, cobbler, and whipped cream in hand, she and Abby walked back into the dining room. Isaac had gotten up from the table while they were in the kitchen and was in the living room on the phone. Tassie couldn't hear what he was saying, but from his curt tone, it sounded like he was annoyed with whomever he was talking to.

Abby noticed the same thing if her frown was anything to go by.

As if sensing their gazes on him, Isaac glanced at them. He said something to the person on the phone, then hung up and walked over to take a seat beside Abby.

"Everything okay?" Abby asked.

He smiled at her. "Everything's fine. It was just a client."

Abby nodded, returning his smile as she went about serving the blueberry cobbler.

As Tassie dipped her spoon into the sweet blueberries, crumble topping, and whipped cream—making sure to get a little of everything—she noticed Isaac seemed preoccupied. Whatever that phone call had been about, it must still be on his mind.

Her mom's cobbler was delicious, as always, and within minutes, they were all talking and laughing again, Isaac included.

Tassie and Baxter left a few hours later, saying she needed to stop at Pupcakes to put away the doggy treats she'd made and left out on cooling racks before coming over for dinner.

"Thanks for dinner," she said as her mom and dad walked her and Baxter to the door.

"Be careful helping Jack investigate Juniper's murder," her mom said.

"I will," she promised.

"And don't do anything dangerous," her dad added.

"I won't," she assured them.

As Tassie gave them both a hug, she glanced at the framed photo on the wall in the entryway of her, Abby, and Nolan when they were kids. It was taken the summer before her brother had left Bluewater Bay, and she couldn't help smiling a little as she remembered that day. They'd gone to the park with their parents to see the lobster boat races and spent the afternoon eating funnel cake and ice cream and watching to see if their favorite boat would win. Looking at it made her happy and sad at the same time.

And even more determined to find out what had happened to make her brother leave town.

Chapter 19

Bluewater Bay was as sleepy after ten o'clock on a Friday night as it was on the weeknights—at least in the part of town near Pupcakes. The area near the microbrewery and nightclub was busier, of course, but they weren't anywhere near the doggy bakery, so it was pretty quiet as Tassie and Baxter got out of her SUV and walked up to the door.

She slipped her key into the lock, but before she could even turn it, the door swung open. She frowned. That was odd.

"Did I forget to lock up when we left?" she asked Baxter.

Her fur baby didn't look at her. Instead, he let out a soft, little growl as he focused on the door.

"Yeah, I know. I can't believe I forgot either."

She must have been so preoccupied with having dinner at her parents that she hadn't realized it. Even so, she was sure she'd closed the door. Frowning, she pushed it open all the way. Her pup scooted in ahead of her instead of staying beside her like he usually did, barking like crazy.

"Baxter, what on earth…?"

The words ended in a startled scream as someone darted out of the break room and ran past them at a dead run, shoving her aside as they rushed from the shop, almost knocking her down. By the time she regained her feet, the intruder was nowhere in sight.

Heart pounding, she slammed the door and locked it as Baxter frantically looked out the window, searching for whoever had broken into the shop. Turning on the light, she pulled her phone out of her crossbody bag with shaking hands and called Jack.

"Hey," he said.

"Jack! Someone just broke into Pupcakes!"

He muttered something she couldn't catch. "Are you and Baxter safe?"

"Yes," she said. "Whoever it was ran out when we came in and I've got the door locked."

"Good. I'll be there in five minutes."

Slipping her phone back into her bag, she reached for Baxter, picking him up and cuddling him. "Come here, baby. Jack said he'll be here in five minutes."

He made it in three. Which had her wondering if he'd been at the station this late or whether he lived that close to town.

Tassie would have asked when she unlocked the door and let him in, but he spoke before she could say anything.

"Are you guys okay?"

Better now that he was there. But she didn't say that. He searched her face with his gaze, then looked her up and down, like he was checking for injuries.

"We're okay."

"Were you here when the person broke in?"

She shook her head. "No. Baxter and I stopped by after having dinner at my parents' to put away the treats I left out to cool, and when we got here, the guy came out of the break room and ran out the door."

Jack studied the door for a moment, then bent to inspect the lock before standing up again. "This was picked by someone who knew what they were doing. Are you sure it was a man?"

Tassie thought about it, trying to remember what she'd seen. "I hadn't turned on the lights yet, so it was kind of dark, but the person was pretty big and moved like a man, so yeah, I think so."

Jack closed and locked the door. "Did he take anything?"

"I'm not sure. Most people pay by debit or credit card, so we don't get a lot of cash, but any we do, we take out of the register when we close up for the day, so there wasn't any money for him to steal," she said. "We haven't gone into the break room yet, though I'm not sure what he would have been looking for in there."

Turning, she and Baxter led the way toward the back of the shop.

Tassie wasn't sure why, but from the way the intruder had run out of the break room, she expected it to be a mess, so she was surprised to see that it looked exactly like it usually did—with one small exception. The drawers of the small desk up against the far wall were hanging open, the stuff inside clearly rifled through.

Like someone had been looking for something they really wanted.

But what?

"Do you keep anything important in there?" Jack asked, wandering over to stand beside them.

"Just pens and pencils, notebooks and paper clips. Stuff like that."

He frowned. "Well, whoever broke in probably wasn't looking for that kind of stuff. Don't touch the desk or anything in the drawers. I'll get someone over here as soon as you open the shop tomorrow to check for fingerprints. The intruder probably wore gloves, but maybe we'll get lucky."

Tassie hoped so.

Jack looked around the break room, his gaze coming to rest on the murder board. His mouth curved as he read what she'd written.

"You got a lot done since this afternoon," he remarked. "This looks good."

"Yeah. Baxter and I worked on it after we had lunch with you." She turned to face him, arms folded. "Wait a minute. I thought you didn't like murder boards."

"I never said I didn't like them. I said I didn't use them," he corrected. "I like yours."

The compliment made her smile.

Jack, on the other hand, suddenly turned serious. "As much as I value your insight, I don't think you should investigate this case anymore."

She blinked. "What? Why not?"

"Because whoever broke in tonight could be the murderer," he said.

"Why would the murderer break in?"

The look he gave her made her think he thought that should be obvious. It wasn't.

"To scare you. To hurt you. To warn you not to keep digging."

"To search my desk?"

He gave her a dark look. "That isn't funny."

"I'm not trying to be," she said. "Jack, I can't stop investigating Juniper's murder, especially not when two of my friends are suspects. Besides, I want justice for Juniper."

Tassie hadn't meant to use the hashtag her fans were using on social media. She'd said it without thinking. But the sentiment was genuine. Juniper *did* deserve justice.

Jack only scowled.

"Besides," she added. "If this was somehow meant to scare me off looking for the murderer, then why run out when Baxter and I came in? And why break into Pupcakes when it was closed and he knew I wasn't here."

Jack considered that.

"Maybe they didn't want to scare you off. Maybe whoever it was wanted a look at this," he said, gesturing to the murder board.

"That doesn't even make any sense," she protested. "How would whoever it was have known this was here?"

Jack didn't seem to have an answer to that.

Tassie sighed. "Jack, it'll be fine. I have Baxter to protect me."

While that was definitely true, Tassie wouldn't let Baxter do it. If they were in danger, she'd do whatever she had to do to protect her fur baby.

"But it won't come to that because I don't think this is related to Juniper's murder," she insisted. Unfortunately, she didn't know what it was about. Bluewater Bay didn't have break-ins. Then again, they never used to have murders either. "Maybe the guy who broke in was looking for money and thought he'd find it in the desk since there wasn't any in the cash register."

Jack's mouth tightened, but he didn't say anything.

"I need to put the doggy treats away," she said.

Turning, she walked out of the break room and into the main part of the store, heading for the kitchen area and the treats still on cooling racks, Baxter prancing right along with her. Jack followed, folding his arms as he watched her place the treats in a container.

"My mom mentioned that one of their vet techs is a friend of Victoria," Tassie said after a few moments of quiet. "She told Mom that Juniper promised Victoria she would help her launch her career, but never did. That certainly gives Victoria motive, don't you think?"

He nodded. "Definitely. Especially considering how quickly Victoria took over Juniper's YouTube channel and is making it her own."

"That's what I thought." She flashed him a smile. "See how well we work together?"

"I never said we didn't. But I can't help worrying about you and Baxter."

The concern in his voice and mirrored on his face made her breath catch. "We'll be careful. I promise."

"That's all I ask. Thank you."

They were both quiet for a while as she placed a few more treats in the container.

"I think I figured out how to get Gwen and Irene in the same place at the same time," she finally said. "I'm going to tell each of them that I want to try to adapt some of their recipes into doggy treats, then refuse to let either of them leave until they talk it out."

"That could work," he said. "Let me know if you need me to post an officer at the door to keep the peace."

She laughed. "I will."

"So," he said after a moment. "How did dinner at your parents' go?"

"Surprisingly fun. Usually, my mom and dad are super quiet when we get together for my brother's birthday, but tonight, they were talking and laughing and everything. Abby and I had planned to talk to them about Nolan to see if they'd tell us anything, but we were having such a good time, we decided not to ruin the evening. My mom and dad get upset whenever we mention him."

Jack watched as she closed the container, then stowed it on the shelf before putting away the racks. "Do you want me to see if I can find your brother?"

Sitting on the floor beside her, Baxter gazed up at Tassie curiously.

Tassie didn't answer right away. Part of her wanted to say yes, but the other part was afraid to. She'd scoured the internet for mention of her brother, hoping that he was living his best life somewhere and she'd find a Facebook Page or something, but she'd come up empty. Not everyone was on social media, of course—especially if they didn't want to be found. But what if Nolan wasn't on social media because her brother was dead? Having Jack do some digging could confirm that fear, and she wasn't sure she wanted to know.

"I'm scared of what you'll find out about Nolan," she whispered. "Can I think about it?"

He gave her a warm smile. "Of course."

They left the shop a few minutes later, Jack saying he'd follow to make sure she and Baxter got home safely. Tassie wasn't sure that was necessary, but she appreciated it anyway. She was a little surprised when he said he wanted to do a quick check of the townhouse she and Baxter shared with Abby and Finn to make sure no one had broken in and was waiting for them, especially since her sister wasn't home.

"You don't think...?" She let the words trail off.

"I don't know," he said. "Which is why I want to check."

Tassie nodded, waiting in the entryway with Baxter while Jack searched the house. Since her fur baby didn't act like anyone was there, she was pretty sure Jack wouldn't find someone, but she let him look anyway.

"All clear," Jack said when he came back downstairs. "Lock the door and don't open it to anyone. And if you hear anything suspicious, call me right away. Don't go looking to see what it is. Okay?"

Her lips curved. "Okay. Thank you."

His gaze was warm. "Have a good night."

"You, too."

He glanced at her fur baby. "Baxter."

It wasn't until Jack left and she'd locked the door that Tassie realized she should have asked him if he wanted to stay for tea. Decaf at this time of night, of course.

Tassie looked down at Baxter. He looked like he'd been thinking the same thing.

"What's that saying? You snooze, you lose?" She sighed. "Yeah."

Chapter 20

"What is *she* doing here?" Gwen demanded.

The *she* in question was Irene, and Gwen clearly wasn't happy to see her at Pupcakes when she walked into the shop the next day.

Standing over by the counter in the kitchen area, Irene folded her arms with a glare. "*She* would like to know the same thing about *her*."

Tassie stifled a groan. When she'd asked Gwen and Irene to come by the store after closing, she'd known what their reaction to seeing each other would be, but it was still frustrating.

"I thought you asked me here to talk about making some of my recipes dog-friendly," Gwen said, turning accusing eyes on Tassie.

Irene stopped glowering at Gwen long enough to frown at Tassie. "You asked me to come by for the same thing."

Great. Now, they were ganging up on her.

Tassie held up her hands placatingly. "I might have fibbed a little about that, but it was the only way I could think of to get the two of you in the same room."

"Why?" Gwen snorted. "So we could kill each other?"

Tassie groaned again—out loud this time. Beside her, Baxter looked back and forth between Gwen and Irene like he was trying to decide if they just might try to murder each other.

"No one is killing anyone," Tassie said firmly. "And if you try, just remember I have Jack on speed dial."

Gwen and Irene both made faces at that.

"So, why did you want us in the same room, as you put it?" Gwen asked, folding her arms.

"When I asked what happened between you and Irene back in high school, you told me to talk to Irene, so I did," Tassie said.

Gwen slanted Irene a hard look. "And what did she tell you?"

"That you think she was why you didn't get to go to Paris," Tassie said.

"I *think* that because it's true."

Irene rolled her eyes. "You're delusional."

"And you're a backstabber!" Gwen snapped.

Tassie exchanged looks with Baxter before turning back to her friends. Sometimes, they were exhausting.

"That's enough. Both of you," she said firmly. "Gwen, Irene didn't steal your registration."

"Yes, she did!"

"No, she didn't."

Gwen lifted her chin. "How do you know that?"

"Because Wyatt took it."

Irene did a double take at that but didn't say anything.

Gwen frowned. "My high school boyfriend? *That* Wyatt?"

"Yes," Tassie said. "*That* Wyatt. He admitted it to me."

Gwen stared at Tassie for what seemed like a whole minute. "I don't believe that. Why would he steal it?"

Irene let out a snort. "Oh, so you believe I'd steal it, but not Wyatt?"

Afraid the comment would get them arguing again, Tassie quickly jumped in before Gwen could say something snarky in return.

"Wyatt took it because he didn't want you to go to Paris," she said. "He was afraid you'd meet a guy there and break up with him."

Gwen was quiet as she tried to wrap her mind around that. "But I broke up with him anyway."

She looked at Irene. After a moment, realization slowly dawned on her face, followed quickly by chagrin as she looked at her friend.

"Irene, I..." she began.

But Irene didn't let her finish. "Don't you dare say you're sorry because I don't want to hear it."

Gwen took a step toward Irene, eyes pleading. "But I *am* sorry. I never should have accused you."

"You're right," Irene said. "You shouldn't have. And I don't know if I can forgive you."

Gwen caught her lower lip between her teeth, hurt reflected in her eyes.

Irene looked away, staring down at the floor.

Tassie had hoped that after Gwen learned about Wyatt ruining her chance to go to Paris, it would mend her friendship with Irene. That once Gwen apologized, Irene would forgive her. But now, Tassie wasn't so sure. She glanced at Baxter, wondering if he had any ideas. He gazed up at her for a moment, then looked at her friends before turning his attention back to her, as if to say,

This was your idea. Do something before Gwen and Irene both walk out of here!

Baxter was right.

As always.

But what could she say to convince Irene?

"Irene..." Tassie began.

Irene lifted her head to glare at Tassie. "Don't tell me that you're taking her side!"

"I'm not taking anyone's side. I'm trying to help you and Gwen remember that you used to be best friends. That you used to spend hours together coming up with new recipes for cookies and cakes and brownies, then baking each of them to see if they tasted yummy enough to enter in the summer and winter festivals," Tassie said. "I know Gwen hurt you, Irene, and I'm not asking you to forget what she did. But I am asking you to forgive her."

Gwen regarded Irene expectantly, waiting for her to say something, but Irene was stubbornly silent.

Tassie sighed. "I get it. If I were in your position, maybe I'd hate Gwen too much to forgive her, too, but just think about it, okay?"

"I don't hate Gwen," Irene said softly.

Tassie did a double take. Well, she'd really misread that.

Gwen seemed even more surprised. "You don't?"

Irene shook her head, gaze on Gwen. "I never hated you. I was furious with you. And part of me probably still is. But I've missed hanging out with you and I want to be friends again. It's just that after everything that's happened, I don't know how to take that first step."

Tassie grinned. "I think you've already taken it."

Gwen and Irene looked at each other for a moment before rushing forward to hug.

Baxter smiled up at Tassie. She smiled back. Yeah, she was happy—and relieved—this had worked out, too. For a minute there, she'd thought this whole thing was going to end up being a disaster.

When Gwen and Irene pulled away, they both turned to Tassie.

"Thank you," Gwen said. "We would never have made up if you hadn't brought us together."

"I'm just glad I could help. Seeing the two of you fight has been exhausting," Tassie said. "And now that you're back to being friends again, Graham can finally ask Gwen out."

Tassie wasn't sure who was more stunned at that, Gwen or Irene.

"Graham likes me?" Gwen asked.

"My brother likes her?" Irene stammered.

Tassie laughed. "Yes! I can't believe neither of you knew that. Graham crushed on Gwen all through high school but was always too shy. He's wanted to ask her out ever since we all graduated but didn't because he was afraid to hurt Irene."

"Oh, man," Irene moaned. "Now I feel even worse about this whole misunderstanding."

"Me, too." Gwen looked equally upset, but then brightened. "But that's in the past. If Graham asks me out, I'm definitely saying yes. I've always liked him."

Tassie was pretty sure that after Graham learned they were once again friends, he'd ask Gwen out. Baxter seemed confident, too.

"You know," Irene said with a grin, looking at Tassie. "When you asked me to come over to make some of my recipes dog friendly for Pupcakes, I was pretty psyched. You still want to do that?"

"I'm with Irene," Gwen said. "If you're game, I am too."

Tassie glanced at Baxter, who seemed to think that was a wonderful idea, if the expression on his cute, furry face was any indication.

"Let's do it!" she said. "What do you say we go to The General Store and have dinner while we talk?"

Gwen and Irene both bobbed their heads excitedly.

"I'll go get Baxter in his harness and grab my purse," Tassie said.

It wasn't until they got to the restaurant that she remembered what Irene had said about not knowing how to take that first step in mending her relationship with Gwen. Was that why Nolan hadn't come back to Bluewater Bay? Because he didn't know how to take that initial step?

If that was true, then she might have to reach out to him.

But first, she'd have to find her brother.

Chapter 21

Monday was always the least busy day at Pupcakes, so Tassie and Baxter went to the dog park after lunch. The dog park was right on the coast and today the water was teeming with sailboats and kayaks. But as much as she loved watching them navigate the water, it was the stately Indigo Point Lighthouse that was the star of the show. Not only because it was beautiful, but also because it was home to a herd of cute harbor seals that hung out on the rocks sunning themselves during certain times of the year. It was one of her favorite things about living in Bluewater Bay.

There were a few people and their dogs in the park, including Estelle and her Corgi, Snickers, who was wandering around the big enclosure sniffing the grass. Estelle looked up from the book she was reading the moment Tassie and Baxter navigated through the double gate system—it was kind of like an airlock on a spaceship where you closed the gate to the outside, then opened the gate to the park itself—and immediately waved as Snickers waddled over to greet them.

Tassie smiled and returned her wave, then bent to take Baxter's leash off his harness so he could play with Snickers while she walked over to join Estelle on one of the benches.

"I heard about the break-in at Pupcakes the other night," Estelle said, slipping her romance novel into her purse to focus on Tassie. *Oooh. The hunky guy on the cover was certainly handsome.* Tassie would have to remember to ask her if the book was any good. "Did they take anything?"

"Thankfully, no. I think Baxter and I scared him off."

Estelle's eyes went wide. "You and Baxter were there when they broke in?"

Tassie shook her head, explaining she had to put away some treats that she'd baked earlier.

"Thank goodness, you and Baxter are okay," Estelle said.

She nodded. "It was probably someone looking to see if we had anything in the cash register."

Though why the guy thought they kept money in the desk in the break room was still a mystery.

"It still must have been frightening," Estelle said with a shudder.

Tassie *had* been a little freaked out. Not as much as her parents though. Her mom and dad had made her and Abby promise not to go to the shop that late at night anymore. Since she and Abby didn't go to Pupcakes after hours all that often, they'd both readily agreed.

"Did Detective Sterling find out who broke in?" Estelle asked.

"Not yet. But I'm sure he will."

Estelle gave her a knowing smile at the mention of Jack.

Sure she was blushing, Tassie quickly glanced over to check on Baxter. He and Snickers were nearby in the playground area taking turns chasing each other through agility tunnels there. Even though the park was spacious, thankfully, her baby never ventured far from her.

"Estelle," she said, turning her attention back to the woman. "What do you know about my brother?"

Estelle looked at her sharply. "I assume you mean the brother that left town about fifteen years ago? The one that nobody likes to talk about?"

"That's the one," Tassie said. "All I know is that he left in the middle of the night when I was a kid. I was hoping you might be able to fill in some of the details since my parents won't."

Estelle turned to watch Baxter and Snickers. "I wish I could, but unfortunately, that was before I moved to Bluewater Bay. Since then, I haven't heard much more other than what you just told me." She looked at Tassie. "What makes you think I'd know something about it?"

Tassie smiled. "Because no one knows more about what goes on in Bluewater Bay than you."

Estelle beamed at the compliment but then gave her a rueful look. "While that *is* true, I can't tell you anything about your brother and why he left. I'm sorry."

"It's okay," Tassie said, trying not to let her disappointment get the best of her. She'd thought that if anyone knew something about Nolan, it'd be Estelle. "Speaking of things going on in Bluewater Bay, what can you tell me about Juniper?"

Estelle's mouth curved a little at the question. "I was wondering when you were going to get around to that."

Tassie wasn't sure if she should be offended or not. "Is it that obvious?"

"Just a little." Estelle laughed. "But that's because I know you're helping Jack investigate Juniper's murder. I figured you'd track me down at some point to ask if I heard any good gossip that might help."

"And do you?"

"I might. One thing I can tell you for sure is that Juniper thought she was better than everyone else in town. She was quite full of herself."

"Because she was famous?"

Estelle nodded. "And she didn't let anyone forget it. I'm telling you, if I had to hear about that YouTube channel of hers again, I was going to scream. Not that I wanted her dead, of course."

"Of course not," Tassie agreed. "Did you know Juniper well?"

"We saw each other around town, but we weren't what I'd call friends."

Tassie glanced at Baxter and Snickers. They'd gotten tired of the agility tunnels and were now running up and down the various ramps.

"What about Juniper's relationship with her husband?" she asked.

"Calvin?" Estelle shrugged. "They had their problems if that's what you're asking. But then Juniper's relationship with her daughter was rather rocky, too."

Tassie sat up straighter. "How so?"

Estelle did the same, turning on the bench a little so they were almost facing each other, her eyes bright with excitement. Estelle did love her gossip. Which was lucky for Tassie.

"Word is, Elena was going to expose Juniper as a fraud."

Tassie frowned. "A fraud?"

Estelle bobbed her head. "Apparently, Elena was going to tell Juniper's fans that Victoria was the real star behind the channel. Victoria did everything for her but got none of the credit."

"Yeah, I heard that about Victoria, too." Tassie thought a moment. "But how did Elena go from exposing her mother as a fraud to murdering her?"

And if Elena's goal was to get her mother back, putting Juniper on blast for the whole world to see probably wasn't the way to go about it.

Estelle let out a sigh. "That I don't know. It doesn't make much sense, does it?"

"No, it doesn't," Tassie agreed, still trying to wrap her mind around the woman she'd talked to at Hug in a Mug deliberately hurting her mother's career much less killing her. "What about Calvin? You don't happen to know if he started seeing Hazel again, do you?"

"His high school sweetheart?" Estelle frowned. "No. But I did see them talking at Hug in a Mug the day before the *Cupcake Combat* taping. I'm not sure if that means anything though. I do know that Juniper hired a private investigator a few weeks before she was murdered if that's any help."

Tassie did a double take. "Wait. What? Do you know why?"

Estelle shook her head. "Unfortunately, no."

Drats.

"I don't suppose you know the PI's name, do you?"

There couldn't be that many private investigators in Bluewater Bay, but if Estelle knew who it was, then it would be easier to track him—or her—down.

"Todd Knight," Estelle said. "He's in Cutler's Cove."

Tassie grinned. "You do know everything about everyone."

Estelle gave her a smile that would have made the Cheshire cat proud.

"I'm going to stop by and tell Jack about the PI," Tassie said, getting to her feet. "Thanks for the info."

"Anytime," Estelle said. "And if I learn anything about your brother, I'll let you know."

Chapter 22

Jack was chatting with Lucy at her desk when Tassie and Baxter walked into the police station fifteen minutes later. They both smiled as she and Baxter headed their way.

"Hey!" they said in unison.

"What's up?" Jack added.

Tassie returned their grins. "I think I might have a lead in Juniper's murder. It might not be related, but she hired a private investigator named Todd Knight over in Cutler's Cover a few weeks before she was killed."

"Do you know why she hired him?" Lucy said.

"No." Tassie looked at Jack. "But I thought you might want to talk to him."

He nodded. "Definitely. Do you and Baxter want to take a ride?"

Tassie ignored the knowing grin Lucy gave her. She was hoping he'd ask so she didn't have to invite herself. Not that she would have had a problem with doing that, of course. Beside her, Baxter wagged his tail in reply, making her laugh.

"I think that's a yes," she said, then smiled at Lucy. "Oh, and by the way, I'll text Abby and let her know we're going with Jack so you don't have to."

Lucy playfully stuck her tongue out. "You never let me have any fun."

It wasn't until she and Jack were in his SUV with Baxter safely in his car seat and Todd Knight's address was punched into the GPS that Jack brought up her teasing exchange with Lucy.

"What was that thing with Lucy about?"

"She texted Abby the other day to say that you had lunch with me at Pupcakes."

"Um…why?"

"Because she has a ridiculous amount of interest in my love life," Tassie said with a laugh, only half-joking.

Jack smiled in understanding. "Ah."

"Yeah. She actually offered to introduce us your first day of work at Bluewater Bay PD."

He seemed surprised but not bothered by the idea. "What'd you say?"

If she'd known how handsome, kind, easy to talk to, and an all-around great guy Jack was, she would have said yes despite one of her friend's biggest flaws. "I said thanks, but no thanks. Not because of you, but because Lucy doesn't have a very good track record when it comes to introducing me to men. I didn't want her bad luck jinxing anything with a guy I hadn't even met yet."

Especially since he really was as amazing as Lucy had claimed.

"Smart thinking," Jack agreed, mouth twitching as he gave her a sidelong glance. "Lucky for me that she doesn't have a great track record or you'd probably be dating some hunky lobster fisherman she introduced you to."

Tassie laughed. "The most recent one was an electrician, and trust me, no, I wouldn't be. Speaking of dating, do you think I could collect on that raincheck?"

There. She'd done it. *And* fit it seamlessly into their conversation so it wouldn't be weird.

He glanced her way again. "What did you have in mind?"

"I was thinking we could try for Friday night?"

He flashed a grin. "Works for me."

Tassie smiled. Lucy might not be good at setting her up with men, but her friend did give good advice when it came to taking them up on rainchecks. Tassie would have to remember to thank her. "Good."

"We're still looking for whoever broke into Pupcakes the other night, but without any fingerprints, it's going to be difficult finding the guy," Jack said as they left town proper and turned on to the road that would take them around the bay to Cutler's Cove.

Even though you could see Cutler's Cove from Bluewater Bay, thanks to all the inlets, they'd never built a bridge to connect the two towns, so it was a thirty-minute scenic drive along the coast. Tassie had lived here her whole life and was still awed by how beautiful this part of Maine was.

"I figured as much," she said.

"You should get some security cameras."

Tassie dragged her gaze away from the boats out on the water to look at him in surprise. "Cameras? You're joking, right? This isn't New York City."

"And yet someone still broke into your shop."

"Okay, point taken." She sighed. "But do you honestly think security cameras are necessary? That seems kind of extreme."

"Yeah, I do. And it's not extreme," he said. "It's a good way to make sure you're being safe."

She sighed. She supposed that made sense. "Aren't security cameras super expensive?"

"They used to be, but not so much anymore. I can help you pick one out. I'll even set it up for you." He looked at her. "If you don't want to do it for your peace of mind, then do it for mine." When she didn't say anything, he glanced in the rearview mirror at her pup. "Back me up on this, would you, Baxter?"

Tassie half turned around to look at Baxter.

"He's grinning, isn't he?" Jack prompted.

He was.

She scowled at Jack. "How do you know that? You can't even see him from where you're sitting."

"Because I know he agrees with me."

Tassie shook her head with a laugh. "Okay, you win. But I'm going to take you up on your offer to set it up. I don't know the first thing about security cameras."

"Deal," he said, throwing a smile her way. "So, did your source tell you about Juniper hiring a private investigator?"

Tassie's mouth curved. When Estelle had dished to her about the townsfolk while she and Jack had been solving their first murder together, she'd teasingly insisted that an amateur sleuth never revealed her sources.

"They did," she said.

"One of these days, you're going to have to introduce me to your source, you know. Unless they come by their information illegally," he added. "Then maybe you shouldn't introduce me."

Tassie laughed, imagining Estelle having a secret room at the historical society with multiple monitors and listening equipment so she could see and hear everything going on in Bluewater Bay.

"I've been thinking about why Juniper might have hired a private investigator," she said after a moment. "My source mentioned they heard Elena was going to expose Juniper as a fraud and tell her fans that Victoria is the real genius behind the brand. Maybe Juniper hired this PI to get dirt on Elena so she could blackmail her into keeping quiet."

Jack considered that. "So, we're talking like an assured mutual destruction kind of thing?"

She nodded.

"And you think Elena murdered her mother to keep anyone from finding out whatever that dirt was."

Tassie let out a sigh. "After talking to Elena the other day, I don't want to think that, but...maybe."

It seemed incredible to imagine that Juniper's daughter could have killed her, but Tassie watched enough mystery shows and read enough books to know that people committed murder for all kinds of reasons.

She was still pondering that when they got to Cutler's Cove. The town was quaint and cozy like Bluewater Bay, but in a whimsical, almost quirky kind of way. That could be thanks to the peaked arch over the main street welcoming you to town as you drove in. Or maybe it was the gigantic bell buoy tipped on its side in the park near the harbor. Whatever it was, the whole place had a charming vibe to it.

Todd Knight's office was located off the main coastal road, further inland. Tassie had never been to a private investigator's so she wasn't sure what to expect. She'd actually pictured a seedy place in a strip mall between a laundromat and a bail bonds business.

Todd Knight's office wasn't that.

His office was in the bottom floor of a Cape Cod–style townhome with a florist on one side, a sandwich shop on the other, and a lawyer upstairs. The shops in the rest of the townhomes were just as upscale.

Tassie should have known that Juniper would hire someone fancy. Not that she blamed her. Tassie had Googled him on the way over and the guy had excellent reviews.

Knight Investigations was to the right of the entryway, situated in what would be the living room area if the townhome was an actual house. The space had been divided into a small lobby area and an inner office that must be Todd's. The outer area boasted a leafy ficus near the window and a table with one of those fancy coffee machines that made individual cups.

The blonde receptionist seated at the desk gave them a smile as they walked in. "May I help you?"

"We're here to see Todd Knight," Jack said.

The woman looked from Tassie and Baxter to Jack and back again, her dark gaze curious. "Do you have an appointment?"

Jack flashed his badge. "We're here to talk to him about a case he's working."

The receptionist's eyes went a little wide at that. "Oh! Just a moment." Picking up the cordless phone, the woman pressed a button, then waited. "Todd, the police are here to see you." Setting the handset back in its cradle, she smiled at them again. "He'll be right with you."

"Thanks," Jack said. He turned to Tassie. "This is the fanciest private investigator's office I think I've ever seen," he said softly.

"Me, too. Not that I've been in any private investigators' offices, of course," she said, then added, "Unless you count TV."

Jack chuckled and opened his mouth to say something, but the door behind Jack opened and Todd walked into the reception area. Like the office itself, the man wasn't what Tassie expected. Tall and trim, he had dark hair and eyes along with a neat beard and mustache.

"I'm Todd Knight," the man said. "How can I help you?"

Jack held up his badge. "Detective Jack Sterling from Bluewater Bay PD and this is our consultant, Tassie Drake. We'd like to ask you some questions about Juniper Larabee."

"Ah." Todd nodded. "Come in."

Jack gestured for Tassie to follow Todd, falling into step behind her and Baxter.

The white wainscoting that lined the lobby continued into Todd's office, as did the soft blue-gray paint on the walls above it. There was a framed certificate on the wall displaying his license from Maine's Special Investigations Unit as well as black and white photos of various oceanic scenes.

Todd jerked his head toward the chairs in front of his desk as he moved behind it. "Have a seat."

Jack took one chair while Tassie slipped into the other. Baxter immediately jumped into her lap, turning to face Todd, then sitting down and making himself comfortable.

"I understand that Juniper hired you a few weeks before she was murdered," Jack said. "What did she want you to investigate?"

Todd leaned back in his chair. "She was convinced her husband was cheating on her with her assistant."

Tassie exchanged looks with Jack even as Baxter looked over his shoulder at them to do the same. Tassie had thought for sure Calvin was having an affair with

Hazel. Of course, he still could be, depending on what Todd found out.

"What made her think that?" Jack said.

"She said he'd become distant and cold lately. He didn't want to spend time with her like he usually did and had started dismissing things she said. Your standard stuff."

That didn't necessarily mean Calvin was cheating on Juniper. But it could mean that he was planning to murder her.

"Did you find evidence he was cheating on her?" Jack asked.

"Not definitively, no," Todd said. "I started following him right after she hired me and though I saw him with her assistant once, I didn't see anything to suggest they were romantically involved. I took photos if you want to see them."

Jack nodded. "Please."

Todd leaned forward and tapped the keys on his laptop. A moment later, the TV on the wall to their right lit up and a photo of Calvin and Victoria appeared. They were in front of the Larabee home and it looked like they were simply talking. They weren't even standing close to each other.

As the private investigator flipped from one photo to the next, Tassie caught sight of what looked like a very familiar delivery bag in Calvin's hand.

"Can you zoom in on the bag Calvin's holding?" she asked.

"Sure," Todd said, doing as she requested so that the white bag with red writing was front and center.

Tassie turned to Jack. "That bag is from Ayer's Pharmacy. I recognize it from when I worked there as a pharmacy tech before opening Pupcakes. Ayer's uses those kinds of bags when they deliver things like inhalers and auto-injectors to their customers."

"And if there were auto-injectors in that bag, it could directly tie Calvin to Juniper's murder," Jack said.

Tassie bobbed her head excitedly.

This was *huge*!

Jack looked at Todd. "Thanks for the help."

Tassie stood along with Jack and Todd, Baxter chilling in her arms.

"Glad I had something that might help catch Juniper's killer." Todd gave her a smile as he came around the desk. "Who's this little guy?"

Tassie grinned as her fur baby wagged his tail in greeting when Todd reached out to pet him. "This is Baxter."

"Nice to meet you, Baxter," Todd said, his gaze flicking to her. "I don't think I've ever seen a police consultant with her own K9 partner."

She laughed. "We're a team."

Tassie was still trying to figure out if Todd was flirting with her when Jack stepped a little closer to her and Baxter at the same time that he held out his card.

"If you think of anything else," Jack said.

In Todd's defense, he didn't know she and Jack were together, but understanding dawned on his face as he took the business card. And in Jack's defense, he hadn't figured out she was a one-man kind of girl yet. She couldn't hold it against either of them.

"Will do," Todd said.

"Do you get a lot of business in a small town like Cutler's Cove?" Jack asked as Todd walked them to the door.

The private investigator's mouth quirked. "More than you'd think. When secrets are your business, Detective, then business is always good."

Behind her desk, Todd's receptionist's mouth curved into a smile at that.

Tassie would love to know what kind of secrets the people of Cutler's Cove had but decided that the townsfolk of Bluewater Bay were keeping her and Baxter busy enough.

"Are you going to arrest Calvin?" she asked Jack the moment they were in his SUV.

"Not yet. First, we need to check with the pharmacy and make sure that delivery Calvin had was in fact Juniper's auto-injectors. If they were, then I'll bring him in for questioning and try to rattle him, see if I can get him to confess."

She'd been hoping he could arrest Calvin, but bringing him in for questioning worked too, she supposed. Maybe they'd get lucky and the man would admit everything.

"While you're talking to Calvin, I could talk to Victoria, see if she saw what Calvin did with those auto-injectors," Tassie offered.

"No way," Jack said. "It's too dangerous. If Calvin is having an affair with Victoria, she could be involved in Juniper's murder."

Tassie sighed. He had a point.

Drats.

"You're right. I'll go talk to Ada instead," she said after a moment. "If Juniper confided in anyone about her suspicions that Calvin was cheating on her, it'd be Ada. Maybe she can tell us something that will help make a case against him."

Chapter 23

On the way back from Cutler's Cove, Tassie and Jack stopped by the pharmacy to confirm that Ayer's had indeed delivered auto-injectors to Juniper's home the day Todd took those photos. It took the pharmacy tech a few moments to find the information on the computer, but once he did, they discovered that their suspicions were right. After that, Jack dropped Tassie and Baxter off so she could go over to Ada's place while he brought Calvin in for questioning.

The route to Ada's house took her and Baxter past the high school and Tassie slowed when she spotted her former teacher's car in the parking lot. Classes had let out hours ago and Ada's vehicle was the only one there. Tassie wondered what she was doing at the school so late.

Pulling into the lot, Tassie parked in one of the visitor's spaces near the front of the building, then got Baxter out of his carrier in the backseat. It didn't occur to her that the door of the school might be locked until she and

Baxter were already walking toward it, but thankfully, it wasn't.

With only every other fluorescent light on, the school was darker than it had been the other day they were there. She'd never been in the building when it was empty like this, and it was kind of eerie as she and Baxter made their way through the hallways to the culinary classroom, her footsteps echoing around them as they walked. She slowed when they got to the classroom, knocking lightly on the open door before walking into the room so she wouldn't scare Ada.

But the woman was nowhere to be seen.

"Maybe she went to the restroom," Tassie told Baxter.

Leash in hand, Tassie wandered around while she waited, looking at all the cool kitchen equipment. Being a science nerd, she'd especially loved learning molecular gastronomy, a method that was all about combining chemistry with cooking and baking. And Ada taught all the fun stuff. Like how to make chocolate caviar and deconstructed tiramisu.

Tassie was thinking about wowing Jack with her scientific prowess in the kitchen when she heard footsteps behind her. She turned, ready to give Ada a smile.

Only it wasn't Ada who'd walked into the room.

It was Calvin.

Tassie froze even as Baxter let out a soft growl. She quickly bent to pick up her fur baby, wanting to keep him close.

Why was Calvin there?

Did Ada figure out he'd murdered Juniper and ask him to come to the school so she could confront him?

Was that why she couldn't find Ada? Had Calvin killed her too?

A glance to the side showed her that the door on the freezer unit was ajar. Oh, no. Maybe he'd killed her and stuffed her in the freezer!

"What are you doing here?" she said, trying to sound casual.

He gave her a small smile as he moved into the classroom. "I could ask you the same thing."

"I'm here to see Ada." Tassie made a show looking around. "Where is she, by the way?"

"She's around here somewhere."

That was cryptic. And a little ominous sounding.

She was sure of it now.

Calvin *had* killed Ada.

Tassie wanted to ask why he'd killed her. The simplest answer was that Ada had figured out he'd murdered Juniper. Had she also discovered that he was having an affair with Victoria?

As much as she wanted to know, Tassie knew it wasn't smart to confront a murderer, especially if that aforementioned murderer didn't know she was onto him yet.

Besides, she'd promised Jack—and her parents—that she wouldn't do anything dangerous.

"You know, I think I'll just talk to Ada later," she said as nonchalantly as she could. "If you see her, would you mention I stopped by?"

Holding Baxter a little more tightly, Tassie started for the door, but Calvin quickly took a step to the side, blocking her path.

"You know, don't you?" he demanded.

Her heart rate kicked up a notch. "Know what?"

Calvin smoothly reached over and picked up a butcher knife from one of the workstations without even glancing that way. "Don't play dumb. The whole town knows you're helping Sterling investigate Juniper's murder. That's why you're here to talk to Ada."

She licked her lips. "I have no idea what you're talking about or what you think I know, but you're wrong."

"I don't think so," Calvin said, clearly not buying the lie. "You know I murdered Juniper and now I have to kill you too."

Tassie tried not to focus on the knife in his hand, but that was easier said than done. The blade gleamed in the bright overhead lights, taunting her. Even Baxter was fixated on it.

"If you're right, then there isn't any need to kill me because Jack already knows what I know," she hedged.

"Maybe he does and maybe he doesn't," Calvin said. "I'm gambling that he doesn't and am going to give him two murders to solve."

Tassie looked around wildly, searching for something to defend her and Baxter with. *Exactly how was she supposed to do that anyway?* When they got out of this, she should ask Jack to teach her self-defense in addition to installing that security camera for her.

If they got out of this.

Because right now, that wasn't a given.

Her gaze locked on the set of stainless-steel mixing bowls on the counter beside her. Before she could think too much about it, she grabbed them with her free hand and sent them hurtling in Calvin's direction at the same time she ran for the door.

The horrendous clatter the bowls made as they hit the floor was deafening as it echoed in the room, but they did the trick, distracting Calvin long enough for them to escape.

Tassie raced down the hallway, Baxter in her arms, urgently whispering for him to stay quiet so he didn't give away where they were. Turning right at the next corridor, she made a beeline for the exit only to let out a shriek when Calvin darted out of the cafeteria and blocked their path, butcher knife menacingly held out at his side.

Drats.

Whirling around, she sprinted back the way she and Baxter had come, darting into the stairwell and hurrying up the steps. Whenever she watched a TV show and someone being chased ran upstairs, she always thought it was a stupid idea, but she didn't have a choice.

The second floor was where the math and science classrooms were and she frantically tried each door, hoping one of the teachers had left theirs unlocked. When the handle on the door of the chemistry lab turned, she almost let out a cheer—until she remembered there was a murderer chasing them and that any noise would give them away. Ducking into the classroom, she closed the door behind them as quietly as she could, then turned the lock, only to find that it was jammed. Hand shaking, she tried again, but it still wouldn't budge.

That explained why the door wasn't locked.

Did they dare go back into the hall to look for another classroom or stay where they were? The chances of finding another classroom unlocked was slim to none. Better to stay where they were.

In high school, she'd spent a lot of time in the science department, so she knew her way around the chemistry lab even with the lights off and the blinds down. Hurrying to the back of the room, she hunkered down, hiding behind one of the tall lab tables, the sturdy kind with the black resin tops that were resistant to heat and chemicals.

Heart pounding out of control, Tassie dug her phone out of her crossbody bag and sent a quick, desperate text to Jack.

9-1-1 HIGH SCHOOL.

She would rather have called him, but she was afraid that even if she whispered, her voice would carry and give away where they were.

Sliding her cell back into her purse, Tassie cuddled Baxter close again, praying Jack would get there in time.

Chapter 24

At the far end of the hallway, the stairwell door banged open, smacking against the wall.

Tassie jumped, then quickly put her finger to her lips, reminding Baxter to keep quiet. Not that she needed to. He was a super smart pup.

Outside, she heard Calvin's footsteps and knobs rattling as he tried each door along the hallway. When he found the door to this room unlocked, there was no way he wouldn't come inside to check if they were there.

Drats.

Maybe Calvin wouldn't search the whole room.

Better yet, maybe he wouldn't come in at all.

Or give up looking for them altogether.

But that hope was dashed a moment later when the knob turned and the door opened.

Fluorescent light flooded the room, making her blink at the sudden brightness.

Double drats.

Instead of hiding in a classroom, she should have run to the other end of the hallway and gone back downstairs using the steps at that end of the building. But she couldn't change her mind now.

"I know you're in here!" Calvin called.

Tassie hunkered down even more, afraid to breathe as she listened to his footsteps come closer, wishing she could make them invisible right then. In her arms, Baxter's heart pounded against her hand.

Calvin was almost certainly going to find their hiding place.

She needed a new plan.

And some sort of weapon to defend her and Baxter with.

Because she couldn't wait for Calvin to find them.

Reaching out with her free hand, she opened the cabinet under the lab table. She didn't know what she expected to find. A Bunsen burner wouldn't do much good. Neither would a flask or a beaker. That's when she spotted two glass bottles of hydrochloric acid.

Bingo!

Pulling them out slowly and carefully and as silently as she could, she shifted until her arm was under Baxter so that she could keep one bottle in that hand. Holding onto the other with her free hand, she took a deep breath and cautiously peeked around the lab table to see Calvin standing a few feet away. Taking a deep breath, Tassie jumped to her feet and threw the bottle at the floor in front of him as hard as she could.

The bottle broke, sending glass and hydrochloric acid everywhere, including on Calvin's pants and shoes, where it burned through leather and material with a vicious hiss.

Tassie didn't waste any time, running past him as he shouted in pain.

She sprinted down the hallway toward the stairwell with Baxter, the other bottle of hydrochloric acid still in her hand. She was so out of control as she raced down the steps that she almost fell. Halfway down, she stopped, her heart in her throat.

Ada stood at the bottom of the steps, brandishing a cast-iron frying pan in her hands like a baseball bat.

She was alive!

Tassie opened her mouth to tell Ada to run, that Calvin was right behind her and Baxter, and that trying to fight him with a frying pan probably wasn't a good idea, but his voice boomed above them, echoing in the stairwell.

"Ada, stop her!"

Wait. What?!

Ada and Calvin were working together?

Did that mean they'd murdered Juniper together?

Tassie froze, looking from Calvin to Ada and back again. She and Baxter were trapped.

She tightened her grip on the bottle of hydrochloric acid. Throwing it up the steps at Calvin would be tricky. She might not be able to get the bottle high enough up to hit Calvin. Even if she did, he could dart up the steps and get out of the way.

Tossing the bottle at Ada would be easier. Tassie could push past her and be out of the stairwell before the woman knew what was happening. But that meant Calvin would be free to chase after her and Baxter.

She needed to keep them talking until Jack got there.

If he got there.

For all she knew, Jack might be out scouring the town looking for Calvin and not even have read her text yet.

"How did you figure it out?" Calvin demanded.

Tassie pressed her back against the banister so she and Baxter could keep an eye on both him and Ada. The question actually surprised her. Maybe keeping them talking wouldn't be as difficult as she'd thought.

"Juniper hired a private investigator because she thought you were cheating on her." Tassie slid a quick glance at Ada. "Looks like she was right. She probably didn't expect her best friend to be the other woman though."

Ada snorted. "Don't feel sorry for Juniper. Ever since she became famous, she was horrible to everyone, including Cal and me. Did you know that the *Cupcake Combat* people originally chose me to be the local celebrity judge? Well, they did. And when Juniper found out, she pitched a hissy fit. She didn't even know the show was coming to Bluewater Bay until I told her about it. Then she talked them into picking her for the show instead of me. She couldn't stand not being the one in the limelight. I was crushed and she didn't even care. It was infuriating!"

Tassie would be lying if she said she didn't feel sorry for Ada, but that didn't make killing Juniper okay.

"Is that when you and Calvin started seeing each other?" Tassie asked.

Ada's expression softened as her gaze went to Calvin. "No. We started seeing each other way before then."

"How did you keep anyone from finding out?" Tassie asked.

And how long was it going to take for Jack to get here?

"It wasn't easy," Ada admitted. "But we made it work and made sure Juniper never found out. When she told me she'd hired a private investigator because she suspected Calvin was having an affair, I couldn't believe it. We were so careful."

"Well, if it's any consolation, Juniper never suspected you. She thought he was cheating on her with Victoria." Tassie glanced at Calvin. "Why didn't you just divorce Juniper?"

"Because thanks to the prenup she made me sign, if she divorced me for cheating on her, then I didn't get a dime of her money," he said. "I didn't put up with her for all those years to walk away with nothing."

It always seemed to be about the money, didn't it?

"Was it your idea to use peanut oil to kill her?" Tassie asked.

His mouth edged up. "That was all Ada."

"Calvin came up with the idea to tamper with her auto-injectors," Ada said proudly. "What good would it have been to kill Juniper only to have Victoria save her life?"

They were nothing if not thorough, Tassie supposed.

"Enough talking!" Calvin snapped. "If she knows we killed Juniper, then the cop does, too. We need to get out of here before he comes looking for her and her dog."

As Calvin slowly started down the steps, Baxter looked at Tassie, as if to say, *"If you're going to do something with that bottle of acid, now would be a good time."*

He was right.

And since Calvin was the bigger threat, she'd throw the bottle of hydrochloric acid at him.

Taking a deep breath, Tassie tensed, preparing to toss her makeshift weapon when the door behind Ada was yanked open and Jack appeared. He grabbed a startled Ada by the arm and got her out of the way, handing her off to the uniformed officer with him, then leveling his gun at Calvin.

"It's over," Jack told him. "Drop the knife and put your hands in the air. You're under arrest."

For a minute, Tassie thought Calvin would do as Jack ordered, but then he muttered something under his breath and turned to run back up the stairs to the second floor.

Jack immediately gave chase, taking the steps two at a time.

"Should we go help?" Tassie asked Baxter.

Her fur baby gave her a look.

"Yeah, you're right. We'll wait here."

Well, actually, out in the hallway. They'd already spent more than enough time in this stairwell, thank you very much.

Once in the hallway, Tassie set the bottle of hydrochloric acid on the floor, then cuddled Baxter nervously while she waited for Jack to come downstairs. She didn't doubt he could take Calvin, but that didn't stop her from worrying anyway. Baxter seemed just as anxious as she was.

When Jack appeared a few minutes later with a handcuffed Calvin, they both let out sighs of relief. He handed the man off to another uniformed officer, then quickly strode over to Tassie and Baxter, concern evident on his face.

"Are you both okay?" he asked urgently.

Tassie nodded. For the first time in what felt like hours, she was finally able to breathe normally. "Yeah. Ada wasn't in her classroom and when Calvin showed up, I thought he'd killed her like he did Juniper, but it turns out they were the ones having an affair and committed the murder together. Calvin blocked the exit, so we went upstairs and hid in the chemistry lab, then texted you. When Calvin found us, I threw a bottle of hydrochloric acid at his feet and tried to run down here, but Ada trapped us in the stairwell, and then Calvin showed up again."

By the time Tassie was done, she was out of breath all over again.

Baxter booped her cheek with his nose even as Jack gently cupped her shoulders in his hands.

"Hey," he said softly. "It's okay. You and Baxter are safe. Throwing hydrochloric acid at Calvin was quick thinking, and you did a good job of keeping him and Ada talking until I got here."

She nodded, but didn't say anything, too caught up in his eyes. Gaze holding hers, he slowly lowered his head, and she was suddenly out of breath again, for a different reason altogether this time.

When their lips met, the kiss was gentle and sweet and everything she'd imagined, and when he lifted his head, she was a little dizzy. That could have been because she was lightheaded from too little oxygen, she supposed.

Nope.

It was definitely from that kiss.

Before either of them could say anything, Baxter leaned forward to lick her face and then Jack's before giving them his signature grin.

Tassie and Jack both laughed.

"Baxter was very brave when Calvin and Ada were trying to kill us, by the way," she told Jack with a smile.

Chuckling, Jack reached out to caress his ears. "Maybe we should make you an honorary detective."

"What do you think, baby?" Tassie smiled at Baxter. "Would you like a little badge?"

He let out a little yip of approval.

"I think that's a yes," she laughed.

Chapter 25

"To our first official date," Jack said with a grin, holding up his drink in a toast.

Laughing, Tassie gently clicked her glass of white wine with his bottle of beer. "To our official first date."

She and Baxter had spent the day watching the *Cupcake Combat* taping with Jack and Gus, and now, the four of them were having dinner at The General Store. Their pups were currently hanging out by their table enjoying the sights and scents and waiting for their server to bring dinner out of the kitchen.

"Looks like we're not the only ones out on a date tonight," Jack added.

Tassie was pretty sure there were lots of couples who fell into that category on a Friday night, so she followed his gaze to see who he was talking about. She smiled when she saw Gwen and Graham sitting at a table on the other side of the outdoor dining area looking like they were having a wonderful time, his Beagle, Charlie, chilling beside them.

"Well, it's about time," Tassie said with a grin as she turned back to Jack. "Just between you and me, I'm glad Hazel won *Cupcake Combat* instead of Gwen or Irene."

Jack frowned. "Do you think if one of them had won that'd put a rift in their friendship?"

"I don't think so, but I'd rather not take the chance." She shrugged. "Besides, this will give them something else to bond over."

Jack thought about that. "Makes sense."

She leaned forward, resting her forearms on the table while Jack did the same across from her. "That *was* pretty fun today."

"It was," he agreed. "I can't believe I'm saying this, but Fillmore actually did okay up there."

"I can't believe you're saying it, either, but you're right. He did."

With Juniper gone, they'd needed someone to help pick the winner, so the mayor had, of course, volunteered. He'd been way more insightful than Tassie would have given him credit for, commenting on things like flavor, presentation, appearance, texture, and creativity.

"I still think he's a doofus though," she added.

Jack let out a deep chuckle. "Yeah, me too. And thanks to you and Baxter, I don't have to see Fillmore every day to give him daily updates on the investigation. I couldn't have solved Juniper's murder without your help, you know."

Tassie blushed a little at the compliment, while beside her, Baxter grinned up at them. "Well, we *do* all make a pretty good team."

The town still seemed stunned about Ada's involvement in Juniper's death. For some reason, people had already suspected Calvin. Maybe because when it came to murder, the spouse *was* always a suspect. Tassie had to admit that the cold, calculating way the pair had planned and executed the murder was jarring. She couldn't help thinking that if Juniper hadn't confided in Ada about hiring a private investigator, then the woman might be alive right now.

But how could she have known that she couldn't trust her friend?

It was Juniper's daughter that Tassie felt most sorry for. Not only had she lost her mother, but she'd lost her father, too. She wasn't sure Elena would ever be able to reconcile what he'd done or forgive him, family or not.

Speaking of family.

"Remember when you asked me the other day if I wanted you to look for my brother?" she said. "I've thought about it and I'd like you to see what you can find out."

Jack reached across the table and took her hand, gently rubbing his thumb over her knuckles. "Are you sure?"

Tassie nodded. "I'm sure. If Nolan is out there, I need to find him. I need to know why he left."

"Okay." Jack's mouth curved into a smile. "If we're lucky, maybe we'll have a solid lead on his whereabouts by Dog Days."

Which was just a few weeks away. The thought that she might know where her brother was by then made her practically bounce in her seat.

"Speaking of Dog Days, how's your booth coming along?" Jack asked.

"Abby's done a lot of the work already, but now that we've solved Juniper's murder, I can dedicate some more time to it," she said.

"And I can dedicate more time to finding whoever broke into Pupcakes," he said.

Since both Calvin and Ada had denied breaking into the shop that night—and Baxter had confirmed they weren't lying because he and Tassie were in the observation room while Jack had been questioning them—it was still a mystery.

"You know," she said, leaning forward. "I was going to work on my part of the booth this weekend and wouldn't mind the help if you're interested."

Jack flashed her a grin. "You're on. We can install your new security camera too."

Tassie smiled. "It's a date."

Afterword

Tassie and Baxter are back this summer to help their favorite detective investigate a murder at the Dog Days Festival and there are no shortage of suspects!
In the meantime, catch up with Tassie and Baxter when they investigate their first case, the murder of the meanest get-off-my-lawn man in Bluewater Bay in DOG BISCUITS AND DEAD BODIES!

Life couldn't be better for Pupcakes Bakery owner Tassie Drake. (Well...life could always be better, but things were pretty doggone good.) Her sister was handling the mind-numbing paperwork of the bakery, and the long Maine winter was over, which meant more bakery business and more walks in the park with her Chiweenie, Baxter--when she wasn't baking delectably cute doggy treats, that is.

However, discovering a dead body on the way to the dog park was not on Tassie's to-do list. The fact he was the meanest get-off-my-lawn old man in town didn't make it better. The fact Tassie's best friend was being charged with the murder made it worse. And while the town's new detective, Jack Sterling, might be very (incredibly, drop-dead--oops, bad choice of words) handsome, he had the wrong suspect.

It's up to Tassie and Baxter to find the real killer--and there is a town full of suspects--before her friend takes the fall. But staying ahead of a cold-blooded murderer is no piece of pupcake...

About the author

Paige is a New York Times and USA Today bestselling author of cozy mystery, romantic suspense, and paranormal romance. She and her very own military hero (also known as her husband!) live on the beautiful Florida coast with their adorable fur baby (also known as their dog!).

You can find Paige's books in eBook and paperback online and at bookstores everywhere.

https://paigetylertheauthor.com/

www.ingramcontent.com/pod-product-compliance
Lightning Source LLC
LaVergne TN
LVHW041033180525
811591LV00030B/604